The Three Mrs. Monroes Trilogy

I0563761

Penelope
book two

by
Bernadette Marie

Bernadette Marie and 5 Prince Publishing
copyright 2014

This is a fictional work. The names, characters, incidents, places, and locations are solely the concepts and products of the author's imagination or are used to create a fictitious story and should not be construed as real.

5 PRINCE PUBLISHING AND BOOKS, LLC
PO Box 16507
Denver, CO 80216
www.5PrinceBooks.com

ISBN-10: 1631120417 ISBN-13: 978-1-63112-041-1
PENELOPE
Bernadette Marie
Copyright Bernadette Marie 2014
Published by 5 Prince Publishing

Front Cover Viola Estrella

First Edition/First Printing August 2014 Printed U.S.A.

5 PRINCE PUBLISHING AND BOOKS, LLC.

To Stan,
You've been with me through every crisis, bad day, and horrible experience and you're still here. What more can I say? I love you.

Acknowledgements

To Stan and our boys you are the light in my life that makes me shake any darkness.

To Mom, Dad, and Sissy, you are always my foundation on which I forever build my dreams.

To Connie, Clare, Marie, and Grace, you are my clarity when my dream world becomes cloudy. You're my umbrella when it begins to rain.

To June and Sara, you are my knights in shinning armour! You do the impossible and are gracious to accept more.

To my Street Team and Beta Readers, you are the light in the window when I think I can't go on and finish the story I'm working on. You give me that power to create and continue. Thank you.

Dear Reader,

As an author, I am always afraid of the second book. Suddenly you begin to wonder if you know all of the characters enough to continue on with them.

The Three Mrs. Monroes has been such a delight to write. Each woman brings so much depth to the story.

In PENELOPE, we begin to move on and develop this friendship the three wives have started to create. In this second book, we meet Brock Romero, the man Adam Monroe sent to find his Penelope Monroe. The joy in writing this man was his positive feelings for Adam Monroe, for one, and introducing the reader to his family. Sometimes I enjoy the side characters just as much as the main ones. You'll find he comes from a tight knit family where his mother loves to cook—but can't.

Penelope, Vivian, and Amelia are still building their daycare center and also building a family among themselves. Sometimes relationships aren't always romantic. Sometimes they are built between friends— even if they should all be enemies.

I hope you enjoy PENELOPE and look at the end for a sample of the final book VIVIAN.

Happy Reading,
Bernadette Marie

Penelope

Chapter One

God she was miserable.

Heat waves rose off the pavement and the air was thick and still. Penelope Monroe sat on the front porch in one kitchen chair with her feet up on another. With gentle strokes, she rubbed her pregnant belly. She simply couldn't believe how uncomfortable she was.

The smell of paint from inside the house wafted out and she tried not to let it make her stomach churn. She'd been appointed to oversee the two men putting in the new front window. That wasn't much fun at all.

Both of their butt cracks stuck out of their pants and every time they talked they cursed then looked at her and apologized. She wasn't a prude—well not really. She'd heard those words before, even if she didn't use them.

Penelope closed her eyes and wished for a slight breeze. Her head was buzzing with paint fumes, curse words, and the events of the past few months.

It had all started when she'd married Adam Monroe.

His image formed in her head and she let out a small sigh.

Those blue eyes and that blonde hair, he was like a god, she thought. One she'd read about in books. He was a soldier, so his body was chiseled hard and he carried himself—well, like a god.

He'd been a player. She'd known that. The night she'd first laid eyes on him, he'd taken her friend home from the bar. At least he'd had the sense to offer her a ride home before he drove off with Christina—her *ex-friend*. There were explicit details from Christina she could do with forgetting.

That should have been her clue to never even talk to the man again. Easy sex from women you picked up in bars wasn't her style. She'd been a virgin, after all. She'd been saving herself for her husband. It had been Christina who thought differently of that. Christina liked the loud music, the dancing, the beer, and the men. Usually she was considerate of Penelope's feelings when they went out. But that night Christina had gotten caught up in Adam's blue eyes, his hair, his body, and his voice delivering all the right lines.

Penelope figured she was most mad about the evening because she'd been having feelings she'd never had before. She thought, briefly, that had she been given the chance to go home with Adam she'd have done it. She knew she'd have chickened out, but he'd had a way with turning her heart to mush.

But it had been Christina he'd taken back to his place and—well, again, she'd just like to forget that she knew every detail of that night.

She couldn't have imagined that a few nights later, when Christina had abandoned her at the bar for another one night stand, that Adam would walk in and change her life.

The words he used were different than the ones he'd used on Christina. His moves were gentle and that hadn't been a word Christina had used when she'd given Penelope all of her details.

He was a gentleman.

They talked, walked, and dated a few nights. He was sweet when she told him she was a virgin and she was saving herself for her husband. Not once did he make a move or cross the line. Then he said he loved her and that had changed everything.

When he'd asked her to marry him, there had been no hesitation. They'd gotten married and, that night, she gave herself to him.

Penelope let out a breath and opened her eyes. Everything changed in that one night.

She ran her hand over her growing stomach. A small part of Adam grew inside of her, even though he was gone.

The day she'd come to Parson's Gulch was the day they'd buried Adam—the day she'd met one of his other wives and seen the other with his children. She was only one of three Mrs. Monroes. One of three Adam had lied to. One of three who now fought to move past him.

The very thought of Adam's lies still made her sick.

But just because she now detested her husband of only a few months, she couldn't hate the life that grew inside of her. This child was hers and in a few days she'd see the baby for the first time. Adam's other wives would be there too.

She let out a small chuckle which had the window installers looking over at her. Kindly, she gave them a smile and closed her eyes again.

Amelia Monroe, Adam's second wife, had taken her in. She was kind though Penelope was sure she wasn't used to being such. But she'd given her a place to stay and had just friended her when she'd needed someone to care.

Vivian, on the other hand, had taken a little longer to warm up to. But when she had, they'd bonded. Though Vivian wasn't more than ten years older than Penelope, she thought of her as a mother figure, where Amelia was more of a big sister.

Adam's lies had entangled them.

Adam's death had brought them together.

Adam's life grew inside of her.

Penelope opened her eyes and rubbed her aching side.

In just the past week, her stomach had grown so much bigger. It stretched and Vivian was relentless with the cocoa butter routine. She had stretch marks from Adam's other two children and she was going to make sure Penelope didn't suffer the same fate.

More than just her stomach had changed though. A week ago, the entire town changed in fifteen seconds when a tornado ripped through the sky. There had only been a few injuries and no one had died—thank God!

Vivian's home had been totaled and the front window of the century-old house on Main and Pine had blown in. Penelope's car had also been totaled, but she thought she'd fared pretty well in that deal. Her beat up old car, which didn't always run well, had been replaced by her late husband's vintage Mustang.

Penelope had never been one for flashy, vintage cars, but she couldn't help herself—she loved this one. It sat against the curb within view. Oh, she might look sexy in it now, from the neck up. But no one would ever give her a second look when they saw a baby seat in the back in a few months.

Sam Jackson, Adam's lawyer, her boss, and now Amelia's fiancé, pulled tree branches around the side of the house and stacked them near the porch.

"I have the misting fan set up in the kitchen. Maybe you should go inside," he called to her.

"Too much paint."

He nodded as he took his cellphone out of his pocket. He looked at it, smiled, and walked toward her giving the front window a glance first. "Why don't you go in, get yourself a cold bottle of water, and walk upstairs."

Penelope frowned. She knew it was much hotter upstairs.

Sam climbed the steps of the porch and held his hand out to her. "C'mon. Amelia is up there. She just texted me. She has something to show you."

Penelope planted her feet on the floor, took Sam's hand, and stood with an *umph.*

"You start up," he said placing his hand on her back and walking her toward the door. "I'll get you a bottle of water and meet you up there."

Penelope shifted him a glance and walked inside the house.

The heat was nearly unbearable, but she walked toward the stairs and started up them.

Sam had redone every tread and in time, when she wasn't around, they would stain them and the rest of the floors in the century-old house, which they were turning into a daycare center.

Adam's father had donated the house to them. It was a kind gesture, she thought as she neared the top step. He'd been gracious when they'd needed it.

Amelia had come up with the great idea that they take what Adam had and turn it into a business to take care of his children. Amelia hadn't asked for anything in return. But when pushed, she'd mentioned she'd like a gym in the basement.

So far she hadn't stumbled across the secret project Penelope and Vivian had been working on. She seemed to be preoccupied with what she was calling her office upstairs.

Penelope hadn't been upstairs in weeks. It wasn't worth the climb. And now that she was at the top of the stairs and the air was thick and horribly hot, she knew she'd been right to stay downstairs.

Sam was right behind her with a cold bottle of water. He handed it to her.

"C'mon, go in," he said.

"She's been behind those doors for a week. I don't want to be the one who goes in unannounced."

"You're chicken."

"Yeah. You go first. She loves you."

Sam scowled and stepped forward. "Yeah, and I'm the one she punched in the gut when I startled her too. I'm walking with heavy footsteps."

He twisted the knob of one of the closed bedroom doors and pushed it open. Sticking his head around the corner, he pushed it open just a bit more.

"She's afraid to come in. You're not going to throw anything are you?"

Penelope heard Amelia grunt and then the door swung open hard. "Get in here."

Penelope walked through the thick air toward the room and gasped when she walked in.

Amelia, Vivian, and Vivian's daughters were standing in the room with enormous grins on their faces. "Well, what do you think?"

Penelope looked around at the transformed area. They had taken the two bedrooms, which shared a Jack and Jill bathroom, and completely renovated them.

The room she stood in was painted a very soothing shade of pale green. There was a wrought iron bed with a lacy white spread. Over the bed, was a painting that she knew Vivian had found in the basement. An antique dresser and mirror sat against the wall and they'd also added a beautiful armoire.

"This is magnificent," she said with her breath wheezing out. "This is what you've been working on?"

"Yes. You needed a place to stay," Vivian said. "Amelia did almost all of it."

"For me?"

"You and the baby. This is your home now—when the fumes are all gone."

She felt the tears sting, but she tried to hold them back.

"I did that." Emma, Vivian's four-year-old daughter, said as she pointed to the rocking chair. "The Teddy bear. I made it at Build-a-Bear."

Penelope covered her mouth and tears quickly rolled down her cheeks.

"You're such a girl," Amelia teased as she put her arm around Penelope's shoulders. "C'mon, there's more. Try not to cry too much or you won't be able to see anything."

She walked her to the bathroom that joined the two rooms. It was painted a soft brown and all the fixtures had been replaced with modern replicas of older ones.

"This is gorgeous. I can't believe I didn't know you were doing this."

"That would have ruined the surprise. Okay, now you can cry your eyes out," Amelia said as she opened the door that led into the next bedroom."

When Penelope saw it, she did cry harder. The pastel yellow room with handmade curtains depicting tumbling teddy bears hung from the window. Matching bumpers adorned a crib against the wall. There was a matching rocking chair in this room with a teddy bear on the seat.

Ava, Vivian's two-year-old, tugged on Penelope's shirt. "I made that."

Penelope batted her eyes and ran her hand over Ava's braids and smiled. Never in her life could she have expected such love. And to think, these women and children had been jaded by Adam's lies too. But they were there for her and her baby. They embraced her. They loved her.

"I can't…I don't…Oh…" she sobbed.

Vivian moved to Penelope and wrapped her arms around her. "Quit crying. You're going to make me cry."

"I don't deserve this," Penelope said.

"Sure you do," Amelia added.

Penelope looked up to see her standing with her arms crossed over her chest and Sam next to her with his arm around her shoulders. They made a beautiful picture, she thought. Amelia was very lucky to have fallen in love with him.

"You've all been so nice to me…"

"And we're going to keep being nice." Amelia walked toward her and whispered, "Adam brought us together. We are all family now." She took Penelope's hands in hers. "This is the least he could do to take care of you and your baby."

Again, Amelia was being sweet and that nearly made Penelope want to laugh. But she'd learned this side of Amelia was as genuine as the side that liked to kick men's butts.

As Ava and Emma showed Penelope all the parts to *their baby's* room, the doorbell rang.

They all exchanged glances and Vivian shook her head. "I'll get it. It's probably those boobs putting in the window."

Penelope watched her walk out of the room and then, hand in hand, Sam and Amelia walked out too. She looked down at the sisters of her baby and smiled. She'd be okay without Adam there or any other man for that matter. She and her baby were loved. That's all that mattered.

Chapter Two

Brock Romero figured he was in the right place. The Mustang parked on the street was the same one he'd seen a picture of. If he remembered correctly, this was Adam Monroe's grandmother's house. He'd seen a picture of it too.

It had been awkward calling Adam's parents looking for Adam's wife. Mrs. Monroe, Adam's mother, was hysterical. Luckily his father took the phone from him and gave him this address.

The entire town must be doing spring cleaning. There were utility trucks everywhere. Trees were being cut down, yards redone, and lots of work on roofs and windows, he thought as the men on the porch cursed at the glass they were working with.

The front door was open and paint fumes filled his nose. Adam's wife must be redoing the house from top to bottom, he thought.

A woman bounded down the stairs, but she didn't look like the picture he'd seen. Her hair and eyes were dark. She had a scowl on her face when she looked at him standing there in his fatigues, right off the airplane.

"What can I do for you, soldier? Are you lost?"

Her voice matched the look on her face. If this was Adam's wife, everything he'd heard about her must be wrong.

"I'm looking for Mrs. Monroe. Adam's wife."

Her eyes narrowed on him. "In this house you'll have to be more specific," she said through gritted teeth.

Brock moistened his lips. "I'm sorry, ma'am. Um…" This wasn't good. Maybe this was the woman he'd talked to on the phone. No, didn't Adam's dad say they'd moved? Or maybe this was his real mother and the other a step-mother? No, she wasn't old enough to be his mother. Well, maybe.

"I don't have all day. What do you want?" the woman asked.

Brock swallowed hard. "Ma'am, I'm sorry. I'm looking for a Penelope Monroe. Adam Monroe's wife."

The woman clucked her tongue and nodded. "What do you want with her?"

"Nothing, ma'am. I mean, I was sent here."

"By the Army?"

"Oh, no. By Sergeant Monroe, ma'am."

The woman stepped toward him and crossed her arms over her chest. "Sergeant Monroe is dead."

The heat was so heavy on him now. His fatigues were insulating him and he could feel the sweat roll down the back of his neck.

He'd been in combat. He'd been shot. And yet, this woman scared the hell out of him.

"Yes, ma'am. I know he died. I held him when he did, ma'am."

Her expression changed. It didn't go soft. It didn't become angrier—it just faded.

Her face went pale and she dropped her arms as two more people walked down the steps and toward the door.

Brock looked at them and then back at the woman in the doorway. "Ma'am, are you okay?"

The man who had walked down the steps hurried to them. "Vivian?" He took her shoulders and turned her toward him. "You're pale."

She darted her eyes toward Brock and then back to the man. "I need to sit down. I need some water. I need to sit down."

The man wrapped his arm around her shoulders and walked her away from the door as the other woman who had come down the stairs moved toward him.

"Who are you?"

She was more direct. She stood with her feet spread, her hands behind her back and her gaze directly focused on his.

"Ma'am, I'm Lieutenant Brock Romero. U.S. Army."

The stone stare on him made him want to snap to attention. This woman screamed military.

"What is your business here?"

"Ma'am, I'm looking for Mrs. Monroe."

She coughed out a laugh. "Be more specific."

What was it about this house? He thought saying Mrs. Monroe was specific enough.

"Penelope Monroe," he said hoping someone would let him see her. He'd traveled across the damn world to find this woman and now he was stuck in the heat and not getting anywhere.

The woman crossed her arms over her chest just as the other woman had done. The noise on the porch had ceased and the two men who had been working on an enormous window were watching him plead for Mrs. Monroe.

"Lieutenant, why are you looking for her?"

"I was asked to."

"Who sent you?"

"Sergeant Monroe, ma'am."

This woman didn't go pale when he said his name. Instead, her eyes grew a darker shade of brown and narrowed on him.

"He's dead."

Brock sucked in the thick air. "Yes, ma'am, I know. I held him when he died."

Her arms dropped just as the other woman's had, but she remained stationed in the doorway. "Adam sent you to find Penelope?"

"Yes, ma'am."

"When did he do that?"

Brock shifted uncomfortably. The sweat trickled down the back of his shirt and he realized that once he'd hit the soil in Oklahoma, he was a civilian again. His days in active duty were over. If he needed to wipe the sweat from his brow, he could damn well do it. So he did.

"Ma'am, Sergeant Monroe died in my arms. In his final moments, he asked me to find his wife and…" He stopped. His information was for Mrs. Monroe. There was no need to break confidentiality and tell this woman what Sergeant Monroe had asked him to do.

She leaned her head toward him as if she were waiting for him to finish.

"Ma'am, do you know where I can find Penelope Monroe?"

"I'm right here." An angelic voice spoke from behind the woman blocking the doorway.

A moment later he saw the woman's face from behind the guard. This was the woman he'd seen in pictures. This was the woman he'd been sent for. This was the woman who he, himself, had dreamed of for months.

The woman at the door shifted a look at Penelope and then back at Brock. "He wants to talk to you."

"Okay, then."

The woman looked at him again and narrowed her eyes further. "I'll be just in the other room. I'm a registered weapon, soldier, and I will detain you if I have to."

"There will be no need, ma'am."

She gave him a nod and walked back into the house.

As she moved, Brock got the first sight of Penelope Monroe and his heart sank. It shouldn't have been a shock, really. He knew she'd be pregnant, though in his mind she wasn't, so he'd neglected to imagine her looking as she did. What he was more surprised about was the fact that even with her slightly swollen stomach she was still beautiful and that was doing strange things to him.

Penelope held her hand out to him. "I'm Penelope."

"Romero. Brock Romero, ma'am," he said as he shook her hand.

She smiled sweetly, just as she had in the photographs he'd seen of her. "You don't have to address me like that. I'm not old enough to be a ma'am."

"Yes, ma'am." He cringed. "I mean, okay."

She stepped toward him. "Can I offer you a drink? We don't have much. But I have some cold water in the kitchen."

He was dying on the porch and sure could use some water, but the thought that the kitchen might be filled with those people who hadn't been very receptive to him didn't enthuse him. However, his need for hydration won out.

"I'd like that, ma..." He tensed. "Thank you. That's very generous."

She giggled and turned to walk into the house giving him a wave with her hand, inviting him to follow.

Brock tried to walk casually, but he wasn't practiced in casual. He was a soldier and letting that slide just the littlest bit was hard. In time, he was sure it would come with ease. But this was new. He'd been a civilian for exactly three hours now. He hadn't even seen his own mother yet. Finding Penelope Monroe had been his main objective since July when Adam Monroe took his last breath in his arms.

When he reached the kitchen with its outdated decor, he sucked in a breath of cool air from a misting fan. But just as quickly the air turned thick again as the eyes of those who had been at the door followed him.

Penelope pulled two bottles of water out of the refrigerator and handed him one. She then looked at the others who were looking at him.

"This is Brock Romero," she told them. "Brock, this is Amelia, Sam, and Vivian."

"It's nice to meet you all," he said.

"How can we help you?" Sam asked.

"I came to see Penelope."

Sam nodded. "Why?"

Brock twisted the top from his water and took a quick sip. He should have answered him first, but the need to wet his mouth was taking over.

"Sergeant Monroe asked me to."

All of their faces were stone hard when he mentioned Adam's name. All of them but Penelope's.

She sweetly looked at the three of them. "Do you mind if we sit in here where it's cool and talk?" She paused for a beat. "Alone."

Amelia grunted. "We're going to be just within yelling distance."

Penelope nodded and slowly the three others stood, gave him a hard stare, and walked out of the room.

"You have more security than the First Lady," Brock said and it merited a laugh from Penelope.

"Mentioning Adam in this house is a very brave thing to do."

"Why?"

"Let's sit down." She motioned to the table.

Brock pulled back a chair and waited for her to sit, then he pulled back another and sat too.

Penelope opened her water and took a long sip. She'd closed her eyes for a moment as she'd done so and Brock watched her with pleasure. He'd had her picture with him for nearly three months. He'd studied that blonde hair which hung in loose curls. The roundness of her cheeks. The fullness of her lips. The blueness of her eyes. And now she was sitting only inches from him.

He never should have studied the pictures as closely as he had. This was another man's wife. She was carrying the son of a fallen soldier—his friend. But it had been a long three months and she'd consoled Brock and she didn't even know it.

As she pulled the bottle back, she let out a sigh and opened her eyes. "It's so hot. If I ever get pregnant again, I'm doing it so I'm not in the middle of the summer with the baby." She laughed. "As if I'll ever do this again."

There was a sadness in her words.

"I'm sorry about your husband," Brock said. "He was a fine man. A fine soldier. He saved my life and I am grateful for that. But had I taken that step, I wouldn't be as missed as he is."

Her mouth tightened. "You were with him?"

"Yes, ma'am." He tensed. "I'm sorry. That'll take some work." He let out a breath. "Yes. I was with him."

"Tell me about it."

Brock wasn't sure that was a good idea. There was no way to paint such a gruesome picture so that she wouldn't lose sleep.

"We were under fire. I'd been hit and Sergeant Monroe was doing his best to lead us out of harm." The scar on his shoulder throbbed and sweat dripped down the back of his neck again. This time it wasn't from the heat, but from the memory that still shook him. "Two more of our men had been hit. None of us fatally, but none the less hit. Sergeant

Monroe got us safely tucked away. He and the others began to tend our wounds."

Brock stopped and took a sip from his water as his mouth had gone dry. "We were still and low for hours. Lieutenant Simms was losing blood and our time was running out. Sergeant Monroe had called for backup and we could hear helicopters in the distance. He'd moved out so we could get to them."

Brock's heart was racing faster now and he fought to still his shaking hands by setting them palms down on his thighs.

It all played in his mind. Sergeant Monroe had ventured out just far enough and then everything went bright and loud. Brock could hear him when it was over and his senses came back to him. The helicopters were overhead. The men moved toward them and he'd moved toward Sergeant Monroe.

He took another sip of water. In his mind he could see Sergeant Monroe lying bloody in his arms. He wouldn't tell her more. But he could see it. Sergeant Monroe's look of shock. He wasn't even sure he knew that his legs had been…well, Brock thought…he was just sure Sergeant Monroe didn't know.

Penelope covered her mouth and he noticed for the first time she had tears in her eyes and they rolled down her cheeks.

"I'm sorry, ma'am. I shouldn't go on."

Penelope lowered her hand to his, which was still on his thigh. She rested it atop his and gave it a squeeze. "No. Please go on."

Brock nodded. He waited for her to move her hand, but she didn't. He took a breath and continued.

"He asked me to pull something from his chest pocket. There was a letter and pictures. Pictures of you," he said as he raised his eyes to meet hers.

"I sent him pictures."

Brock nodded. "I have them in my bag. I'll bring them back to you." She smiled and that hurt him. He'd have to give up the pictures of the beautiful face, which had helped him heal.

"Anyway," he looked down at his hands with hers on top. "He said to find you. You needed to know he loved you."

That had caused her to gasp and when he looked up at her, her eyes had gone wide.

"He said that? Me? He loved me?"

"Yes. He said find my wife Penelope. Tell her I love her. Tell her I love our baby."

Penelope moved her hand and sat back in her chair. She rested her hands on the swell of her stomach and let the tears fall freely.

"He knew about the baby?"

"He'd gotten your letter a few days earlier. We'd all been handed a cigar in celebration. He would have called…"

She shook her head. "I understand."

Brock nodded. "He told me that you needed to know all of this and I should find you. He said he had something in his footlocker I was to bring you. I don't have it with me. It's in my hotel in Oklahoma City. But I'll bring it."

"He loved me?"

Why would she doubt such a thing? He'd flown all this way and had to track her down to tell her. Wouldn't she have known how her husband felt about her?

"I was his last thought?" she asked as if she'd needed validation—again.

"Yes, ma'am." He couldn't help himself. In time, perhaps the ma'am and sir would be reserved, but they were still there.

"Me?"

Again, he wasn't sure why she would question it. "Yes. You. He gave me your pictures and the letter. He said to find you. Though he didn't tell me to look in Oklahoma."

Penelope wiped her tears and nodded. "No. This is new."

"What are you all doing here?" He looked around the outdated kitchen and wanted to laugh at the décor.

She wiped at her cheeks. "Adam's father gave us this house. We are going to open a daycare center here. This way we can have jobs and be with our children."

"He gave it to you and the others that are here?"

"Yes," she said and then let out a sigh. "Adam, well…" She took a moment, rubbed her stomach, and then looked back up at him. "Adam was married before me."

"I didn't know he'd been married previously."

"Still."

What was she talking about? He didn't take her to be dim-witted. "Still? I don't understand."

Penelope adjusted in her chair. "Adam was married to two other women as well."

Now *he* felt dim-witted. As he watched her, he realized he'd sucked in a breath and now held it. He let it out on a cough and just stared at her. "Sergeant Monroe had three wives? You mean he married you and has two ex-wives?"

"No. I meant he was married to all three of us."

"And you knew about that?" Didn't that kind of stuff only happen in Utah, he wondered.

"No," she shook her head. "None of us knew."

Brock closed his eyes. He could hear the explosion and see the white light again. What she was telling him couldn't be true. What kind of man does that? Certainly not a fine soldier. Not a man like Sergeant Monroe.

Chapter Three

What could Brock Romero be thinking, Penelope wondered. His eyes clouded and he'd become quiet. There was some solace that most of the town thought she and Amelia were cousins of Adam's. They hadn't had to face this kind of reaction yet.

"You thought he was a different person, right?" She finally asked when he hadn't said a word.

"I can't judge, ma'am."

She narrowed her eyes, but he didn't apologize. Obviously he was still too shocked.

"You knew him better than I did," she said aloud to herself more than to him. "Certainly there was something in his character that told you he was a..." She stopped. She'd been his defender for nearly three months. She couldn't be calling him names now.

Brock rolled the water bottle between his palms. "He took leave in April. He did say he'd be attending a princess birthday." He smiled and held the bottle in his hands still. "He also said there were some problems back home."

"I'd say."

"When he came back," Brock continued, "he had a new energy to him. He carried a picture of the two of you. He said he'd gotten married. A few weeks after that, you'd sent him pictures of you. A lot of pictures of you. And you wrote to him about the baby."

Penelope pressed her fingers to her forehead. "What happened to the pictures of me? You said you had them? Do you have *all* of them?"

"Just what he carried in his pocket." He leaned in. "I know what pictures you're speaking of. He burned those."

"How do you know about them?"

"Because when he opened the envelope he looked at them, smiled, and threatened any man who moved out of their seats with castration."

Penelope laughed.

"None of us moved," Brock said as he sat back in his chair. "He looked at them. Smiled. And then took a lighter and burned them. He didn't tell us what kind of pictures they were. We didn't ask. But we assumed."

She could feel her face flush with heat. "Okay, we can forget about that now."

Brock nodded and she assumed he was trying to compress a smile.

Penelope took a sip of water. She could hear voices from upstairs and the shuffling of feet. She looked back at Brock. "Did he ever mention that he was married before?"

Brock shook his head. "I only met Sergeant Monroe last December. He made mention once that he had some strained relationships back home. But that was all. He'd write letters all the time, but he never received any from anyone other than his mother. Not until you sent him things."

"He never mentioned his children?"

Brock's eyes grew wide. "Sergeant Monroe has children?"

"Two beautiful little girls. That was the princess party he came home for, I would assume."

Brock's perfect posture sank. "He never mentioned them. They must not have been close."

They weren't, but that wasn't their fault, Penelope thought.

Brock drank down the rest of his water. "I should go and let you get back to work here. I'm staying in Oklahoma City. I have the items to give you in my hotel room."

Penelope nodded and watched as he stood. She moved herself in the chair to stand and he offered her a hand.

"Thank you," she said taking it and hauling herself to her feet.

"I'll be checking out of my hotel tomorrow and I'll come back by if that's okay. After that, I'm headed to Missouri to see my mom. She knows I'm headed back, she just doesn't know when."

"You didn't tell her?"

He smiled and she noticed his cheek dimpled when he did. "I knew I had to find you first."

His words squeezed her heart. A man would really keep his word to another man like that? And she'd married a man who couldn't keep his word to anyone.

"I'll try to stop by before noon." He walked toward the door and Penelope followed him.

He stopped just before the door and turned to her. "I should give you my phone number."

Penelope pulled her phone out of the pocket of her shorts. Brock rattled off his phone number and she stored it in her cell phone.

"If you ever need anything feel free to call me."

Penelope gazed into his rich chocolate eyes. "Why would you do that for me?"

He let out a grunt of a laugh. "I'll tell you tomorrow."

Penelope watched him walk out to the curb and open the door to a rental sedan.

"By the way," he called back. "The Mustang is prettier in person."

"How did you know about the car?"

"That he had pictures of." Brock gave her a wave and a moment later he was gone.

Penelope leaned against the doorjamb, rubbed her stomach, and watched him drive away.

Adam Monroe never talked about his wives and never mentioned his kids, he was courteous enough to burn her risqué pictures, but only bragged about his car. Who the hell had she married?

Penelope turned, her hands still on her stomach. From the moment Brock Romero had talked to her there was something going on inside of her.

She looked up to see Vivian walking down the steps. "Did he leave?"

"Yes. He'll be back tomorrow," she said, moving her hands to different locations on her stomach.

"Are you okay?" Vivian moved toward her.

"I'm fine." She looked up at her. "I think I can feel the baby."

A smile formed on Vivian's mouth and she moved closer and rested her hand on Penelope's stomach. "What do you feel?"

"I don't know. It's constant. Like the baby is jumping."

"I can't feel it, but I'm guessing he has the hiccups."

"I can feel hiccups?"

Vivian laughed. "Yeah. Weird huh?"

Penelope laughed and tears began to burn her eyes. "I've never felt the baby before. But the second Brock came in here I could feel things. Lots of things."

"This is only the start." Vivian pulled her hand back. "So what did he want?"

"Brock? He has something for me from Adam. He'll bring it by tomorrow."

She could see concern flash across Vivian's face. "He's coming back? What does he have?"

"I don't know. He didn't tell me."

Vivian crossed her arms over her chest and the line between her brows grew deeper. "Did Adam send him to talk to all of us?"

Now the quickening feeling she'd felt in her stomach seemed to be in Penelope's chest. "No." She took a breath. "Brock didn't know Adam was married to anyone other than me. He'd never mentioned it."

"Are you kidding me?" Amelia said from the top of the stairs. "Adam never told anyone about his family?"

Penelope looked up at her. "No. He'd never mentioned it or even the girls."

Vivian's face had gone red and Amelia's eyes grew wide.

"Son-of-a-bitch," Vivian growled through gritted teeth. "What a waste of so many years."

Amelia walked down the steps. "Why are you surprised? You don't marry three women without being a man who keeps his own secrets well."

"*I* shouldn't have been a secret. *I* shouldn't have just been forgotten." She lifted her eyes to Penelope. "I sent pictures of the girls every week. I wanted him to be part of their lives and he ignored us. He'd come home and say he didn't realize how beautiful they were or how big they'd gotten. He didn't care about anything. So why would he send someone here to see you?"

Amelia rested her hands on Vivian's shoulders. "Don't jump her. This isn't her fault."

Penelope selfishly wanted to think that it was because he loved her most. Perhaps, for once, someone loved her over everyone and everything else.

The girls walked down the stairs hand in hand. "Mommy, we're hot," Emma said as she waited for her sister to catch up as they took the steps slowly.

"I know sweetheart. But we have to…"

Amelia gave Vivian a gentle shove. "You have to go swimming."

"Are you kidding me?" Vivian retorted as the girls now moved quickly up to her.

"Yeah! Swimming! Please, Mommy."

Vivian narrowed her eyes on Amelia. "Why do you do this?"

"Because you need to spend some time with them. C'mon, look at this place." She swept her arms as if to show her the house. "We're almost done. You've got all the permits and licenses we need. In another couple of months we'll have little kids in here. Your kids. For now, go swimming."

Vivian looked down at her daughters. "You want to go swimming?"

"Yes!" They both answered in squeals and jumps.

"Fine. Let's…" she trailed off and dropped her shoulders. "Let's run to Walmart and buy you a swimsuit."

Penelope felt her heart sink. Most of their belongings were still buried in their collapsed home.

The girls didn't seem to understand their mother's hesitation over going shopping and then swimming, but Penelope did. Everything had a price tag. It cost gas to drive there. It cost money to buy a new suit when they'd probably had a good one back home. It cost time to take away from work. Those were all things Penelope would have heard from her mother—she wouldn't have heard the words, *Let's go swimming.*

The fluttering and jumps in her stomach had eased and now there were just aches in her side. Perhaps it wasn't so much the baby that was making her uncomfortable, but the tensing she did when she thought about her mother.

For a single mother, she'd been very successful. Penelope had been brought up in the best daycare centers, which ran from six in the morning until six at night. That was when one of four teenage girls her mother paid would pick her up, take her home, feed her dinner, and make sure she was tucked into bed. At some point, her mother would kiss her goodnight when she'd drag herself home from the office.

And how did she make it all seem worthwhile? She dragged herself and her daughter to church each Sunday and the word of the Bible was shoved down Penelope's throat until she choked.

She ran her hand over her stomach again. Wasn't that how she'd ended up where she was?

By the time she was twenty, she wanted to experience the world. Her mother had nice clothes, a nice car, a paid off house. What she didn't have was a relationship with her daughter who had walked the line her entire life.

Penelope had made a few friends and learned the joy of going out to parties. Of course, that *walk the line* principle was still instilled deep in her. She didn't drink. She didn't smoke. She didn't sleep with men she wasn't married to.

Air was stuck in her lungs and she fought for the breath she needed. Following all the rules hadn't gotten her very far. She felt the baby again. Her mother had told her how disappointed she was in her for running off and getting married. Her disposition had been even less cordial when she'd told her about the baby.

Well, this baby would be loved and well cared for. This place they were building would be her refuge and her baby's. The baby would have sisters. He or she would have aunties and someday uncles. They were a family and her baby would have a family.

Sam passed by her as the men who had been fixing the window signaled that they were finished.

Amelia touched her arm. "What's going on in that head of yours?"

"Just thinking about things."

"I'm here if you need to talk."

Penelope nodded. "Thank you. I think I should go back and lay down."

Amelia's mouth turned up in a smile. "You could go upstairs and sleep in your own room."

The aches and pains that had tensed in her eased. "That's right. I could."

"C'mon, I'll walk you up."

Chapter Four

The house was quiet. That might take some getting used to, Penelope thought as she lay in the bed and darkness moved in over the house.

She wasn't afraid of old houses. In fact, she thought it was quite exciting to live in a house that had seen decades slip in and out.

What were the stories of the people who lived here? This bedroom—whose was it? Did a small child grow up in this room? A housekeeper? An old grandmother? The thoughts made her laugh.

The baby poked at her and she stopped thinking. Penelope placed her hands on her stomach and felt for that little movement again.

She'd been in love with Adam Monroe. In fact, she'd venture to guess that maybe she was the only one of the three that might still have any kind of feelings for the man at all. But it was hard not to when a little part of him grew inside of her and she could feel it move.

In the morning, she would get her first glimpse of that life. Tears began to sting her eyes when she thought of it. She'd see her baby tomorrow. Hear his or her heartbeat.

Adam wouldn't be there, but Amelia and Vivian would be—her sisters, she thought.

"You're going to be so loved," she whispered to the baby. "And I love you already more than I ever thought I could."

As the tears spilled over her cheeks and down into her pillow she let exhaustion, pride, and love wash over her. Everyday that passed was one day closer to seeing the face of her baby—conceived with the man she loved—and knowing, for the first time, unconditional love.

The next morning, sunlight cast lacy shadows on her walls through the feminine curtains hanging over the windows.

She'd spent her first night in the room Adam's other wives had created for her. What a blessing.

Who would have thought when Adam Monroe took on three wives, secretly, that they would bond? She certainly hadn't thought it when she'd cashed her last paycheck in a daze and drove to Oklahoma.

That had been foolish, she knew that now. But she'd been blindsided by his death. And worse, she knew she was going to face women who would automatically hate her.

Amelia didn't hate her though. That might have saved Penelope's life right there. Had those two women turned on her, she didn't know what she'd have done. Add to it that Adam had left her nothing and their marriage wasn't even legal.

Her breath was coming rapidly now. She was upsetting herself and that wasn't a good thing.

Penelope forced herself to take in a deep breath and let it out slowly. Then again.

Everything, for her anyway, had worked out.

She looked around the bedroom and sat up in the bed. She could build a fresh new start here, in this room with her baby. All of her personal belongings had been destroyed in the tornado. She had nothing left from the life she lived prior to a week ago.

That was okay, she told herself. Nothing had come out of that life anyway. Except, she placed her hands on the swell of her stomach, her baby.

After a few more minutes of appreciating her surroundings, Penelope made her way to the closet and found a few items of clothing. She'd need to go shopping for more, but they'd thought of everything when they'd planned the room.

She took out an outfit and headed to the bathroom to take her shower.

It came as no surprise that the bathroom was stocked with nice things too and a fluffy terry-towel robe hung on a hook.

If it were possible to fall in love with a group of people all at once, she'd done that.

By the time she'd gotten ready for the day, she could smell the scent of fresh coffee and hear voices downstairs. She supposed as long as the voices always came after eight o'clock in the morning there'd never be reason to be startled. The more she thought about it, she realized in another month voices would be heard much earlier that eight-thirty. They'd discussed opening at six-thirty for those parents that needed to be to work by seven. Add that to the pending parenthood she was facing and she was sure she'd never get any sleep.

The thought, or the sheer fact that it was morning had her stomach a little queasy. She sat down on the edge of the bed and caught her breath. Everything was going to work out just fine.

Penelope hadn't been surprised to hear voices, but she was surprised to see that it was Vivian in the kitchen and Brock was sitting at the table.

He stood when he saw her. "Good morning."

"Good morning." She turned toward Vivian. "You're here early."

"Damn tornado. They finally can get me back into my house to collect things. But because it isn't stable, I have to go now. I have to borrow Sam's truck and head over there right now to take out whatever I can." She fumed from the coffee pot to the refrigerator where she pulled out the coffee creamer. "The girls are at the rec center in child watch for the day, which I have to pay for." She poured creamer into her coffee mug. "At least Amelia was able to get me a discount," she huffed as she stirred the cream. As if she'd noticed he was there, Vivian turned and looked at Brock. "I'm sorry. I didn't mean to go on a rant. Things have been a little crazy this week."

"No problem, ma'am. I understand."

Vivian laughed. "You can call me Vivian. I don't need the pleasantries of ma'am."

Penelope laughed and they both looked at her. "Sorry," she said for the outburst as she moved in to retrieve a bottle of water from the refrigerator. She looked back toward Brock to offer him one, but noticed he already nursed a cup of coffee. "I thought you were coming later."

Brock nodded, looked toward Vivian, and then back at Penelope. "I got an earlier start."

The front door opened and she could hear the unmistakable sound of Amelia's walk as she headed their way. "I need your car," she said as she turned around the wall and into the kitchen.

Vivian snapped her head up. "My car?"

"Yes. I have Sam's truck out here for you, but I need to get back to his office and get some files he forgot. What kind of lawyer forgets files for a trial?"

Penelope looked up and her lip quivered so she bit down on it. "The St. Pierre files?"

"Yes."

"They're in the board room, on the credenza. I was walking to his office with them and then I didn't feel good. I set them down…"

Amelia was now right in front of her with her hands on her shoulders. "You're going to make yourself sicker if you keep worrying about this. Now, the files are in the board room?"

"Yes."

"Okay." She turned around and looked at Vivian. "Here are Sam's keys. Give me your keys. I have to head to Oklahoma City."

Vivian pulled her car keys from her pocket and handed them to Amelia.

Penelope moved toward them. "What about my appointment? Will you be back for that?"

They exchanged glances with each other and then both looked at Penelope.

Vivian's shoulders dropped. "Crap! I forgot all about it. I have to go do this. I don't know what I can save, but they said they have to get demolition in there. The lot isn't safe."

Penelope nodded. She wanted to cry, but it wasn't really anyone's fault—though that didn't matter.

Amelia looked at her watch. "I'll try. If I make it back in time, I'll be there. But…"

"I know. I understand."

Amelia moved in and gave her a hug. "You'll be fine. Bring pictures." Her phone rang in her pocket. "I have to go. That's Sam, probably looking for those files."

With that Amelia ran out of the house, the door slamming behind her.

"God, if we have to replace that front door because of her… Vivian winced. "I'm sorry I won't be there."

"It's okay. Really it is." She hoped her voice didn't shake, but she couldn't tell that it hadn't.

"Okay, I have to go. I hope there is something I can salvage in there. I'll get what I can of yours too."

Penelope nodded. "I only had the one suitcase in my room. Everything else was in the car."

They exchanged looks that said they knew that meant Penelope had nothing.

"I'll see what I can find," Vivian assured her, looked at Sam's keys, and let out a grunt. "Bastard left me with nothing and God took away everything else."

"Vivian…"

"I know," she said. "That's not fair. I'm just pissed." She looked up at Penelope. "I'll be there for the next ultrasound, okay?"

Penelope nodded. "I'll be fine."

Vivian rested her hand on Penelope's arm in a sign of sincerity before she too ran out the front door.

Penelope felt the tears begin to sting her eyes and clog her throat. The baby fluttered as if reminding her that they were going to be a team.

She rested her hands on her stomach, sucked in a breath, and pushed back the tears. "I'm sorry I'm a bit of a wreck today."

"It's no problem, ma'am."

Penelope winced. "Please, just Penelope."

Brock laughed. "You're all going to push the boundaries of my disciplines."

"I guess you should give me what you have. It looks like I have an appointment I'll be going to alone." Her voice dropped in disappointment.

"Do you need a ride?"

"I have Adam's car."

"If you just need some support I could go with you. Of course, I could wait in the waiting room, but I'd be happy to escort you."

He did something to her, Penelope thought. His dark eyes, shadow of dark hair, and his deep stirring voice resonated in her. The baby moved again as if giving his or her acceptance to the proposal.

"You'd do that?"

"Of course. Like I said, my mother doesn't know I'm coming. I have time. I'd like to do this for Sergeant Monroe. It would be an honor."

Was it wrong for her to want him there? She felt a connection to him and obviously so did the baby. Perhaps it was that he was there when Adam died. Maybe it was that he was the only person she'd found that respected him and right now she needed someone to believe in him. If for no other reason than to help halt the guilt she felt over loving a man who had done so many people wrong.

"I know we don't know each other, but I'd really appreciate the company. I mean, if you're sure you don't mind."

Brock smiled a million dollar smile. "It would be my pleasure."

Chapter Five

Doctor's offices made Penelope sick. Surely it should have the opposite effect, but sadly it didn't.

She signed in at the counter and then went to sit next to Brock. When she reached him, he stood.

Penelope smiled and sat down before he followed.

"I don't think I've ever met a man so respectful in my life. You'll forgive me if I have no idea how to act."

He sat in the seat next to her. "You should have had men treating you like this your whole life. I tell you what; my daddy would have kicked my back side had I not talked to a lady with respect."

"But you're not around your daddy. And you've been with men for, well I don't know how long. Men don't talk like that when they are alone."

He gave a quick chuckle. "You're right. We don't, but our language and subject matter doesn't have to belittle women."

She nodded with a hum. "I guess you were raised right."

The nurse called her back and as she stood so did Brock.

"I'll be here when you're done," he said with that smile again.

Penelope nodded and followed the nurse back to the room.

The nurse took her vitals and Penelope closed her eyes when she stood on the scale. She wondered if Sam had noticed all of the snacks disappearing in the boardroom. She just couldn't help herself.

Once the nurse had all the information she needed, Penelope gowned as per the nurse's instructions and then lay on the table and covered with the small blanket.

When there was a tapping at the door, she sat up. "I'm ready," she said.

The door opened slightly and she was more than surprised to see Brock peek his head in. "The nurse said I was supposed to come in here. I thought you might have needed me. I can go back out if you want. I don't want to…"

The door opened wider and the doctor was now standing behind Brock. "Please, come on in," the doctor invited.

Penelope looked back at Brock whose face had gone pale, but this was the moment, wasn't it? Why not invite him in? There was no one else to share her joy with, but this man seemed interested enough to have offered to be there with her.

"Brock, come in," she offered.

With a nod to her and then to the doctor, the man who stood well over six foot four trembled as he walked into the room.

The doctor went about getting the room ready and sharing pleasantries of small talk with Penelope, but she couldn't help but be affixed on the man who had barely made it through the door.

His hands were tucked in his pockets as if he were afraid to accidently touch something. He kept his distance as if he still weren't sure he should be there, but he was, and that was more than she could say for anyone else in her life.

Penelope bit down on her cheek. That wasn't fair. Vivian and Amelia had other things they needed to attend to. They would have been there—they would.

"Okay, we're ready," the doctor said. "Just lay back and be comfortable."

Brock had almost made it close enough to the table that she could reach out to him and on a whim she did.

"Come sit next to me," she said softly and he looked down at her.

Had she noticed just how deep and dark brown his eyes were yesterday? She could swim in his chocolate colored gaze. There was a scar through his eyebrow. How had it gotten there, she wondered.

With her hand extended toward him, Brock reached for her and moved beside her. Slowly, he eased down into the chair next to her.

"Okay, here we go. Let's see this baby," the doctor said as he took the bottle of blue jelly and squeezed it onto her stomach.

She jumped and Brock's eyes shot open wide. "Are you okay? Did that hurt?"

Penelope smiled, lost again in the compassion of this man. "It was cold."

"Sorry," the doctor said with a laugh. "It looks like they forgot to turn on the warmer for it. Okay, what can we see?"

The first images began to form on the screen. There were a few bubbles, but nothing that Penelope could make out until...

"Oh, wow!"

She turned her head toward Brock, who was mesmerized by the image on the screen.

She looked back at the screen and there was the image of her baby. Words didn't flow, not even as eloquently as Brock's had. Instead, tears began to pour down her cheeks. There, right in front of her, was her baby.

"It looks like she's sucking her thumb," the doctor said.

"She?"

He gave a little laugh. "Could be he. I was being general. Did you want to know what sex your baby is?"

Yes. No. Did she? This was the hardest question she'd ever been asked. She looked at Brock, but his eyes were glued to the screen.

"I think I'd like to wait. I like surprises."

The doctor gave her a nod and continued on moving the wand over her stomach and clicking buttons on the machine.

Brock had eased in closer now, but she wasn't sure he'd realized it. His one arm rested near her head as he leaned over to see the screen.

As the doctor eased the wand over her stomach and the image of the baby's body appeared she reached for Brock's hand by her side and he gave hers a squeeze.

The tears kept flowing. The baby wiggled and the image disappeared from the screen.

The doctor chuckled. "He's a dancer, huh?"

"Did you feel that?" Brock asked. "I mean, when he moved. Can you feel it?"

She smiled up at him. "Yes. It's like nothing I could even explain to you. It's such an amazing feeling."

One corner of his mouth lifted into a smile and there was a dimple. How could she possibly be so taken by a man she'd met yesterday and laying in such a situation as she was? But there she was, her abdomen exposed, and this man holding her hand. Was there a reason Adam sent him to find her?

She took a deep breath. Okay, now she was being hormonal and sappy. By mistake, he was in this room sharing this moment with her. Nothing more. He'd come to give her something from Adam. He was fulfilling his duty to his superior out of respect.

He'd drive her home, give her the item Adam had sent, and then he'd go to his own mother. That would be that.

She looked back at the screen. The doctor had put the image of her face back up and she was still sucking her thumb. No matter what was to come with her friendship with Adam's other wives or even with Brock Romero, she still had that beautiful face in her life—forever.

As the doctor removed the wand, she began to cry harder.

Brock brushed his hand over the top of her head. "Is everything okay?"

She nodded. "Just emotional."

The doctor wiped off her stomach and pulled up the sheet. "The baby looks perfect. You're doing a good job, Mama." He gave her leg a pat and stood from his seat. "Here's a souvenir." He handed her two photos of the baby. One of his body and the other sucking his thumb.

He extended a hand toward Brock and he stood from his chair. "Take good care of her. We'll see you next month."

"Thank you," Brock said. "Is she okay? Is all of this normal?"

The doctor gave him a pat to the shoulder. "Perfectly normal." He offered her a smile and walked out of the room.

As the door closed, Penelope wiped her tears from her cheeks and Brock plopped down in the chair next to her.

"I didn't expect to be doing this today," he said on an expelled breath.

"I'm sorry you got dragged in here…"

"I'm not," he quickly interrupted. "That had to have been the coolest thing I've ever seen in my entire life."

She smiled so wide her cheeks nearly ached. "Really?"

"Oh, yeah. I've seen men die, but…" He stopped and looked away. "I'm sorry. That wasn't the right thing to say."

Penelope reached for his hand. "It's okay. I'm comforted knowing you were with him when he died. And you offered me great comfort today. I know the girls would have been here if they could have been."

Brock's thumb brushed over her knuckles and it sent a surge through her that was nearly orgasmic. It must have surged enough that the baby moved and she quickly placed her other hand on her stomach.

"Did he move?" Brock asked.

Penelope nodded. "He does it a lot when you're near me. It's like he knows your voice."

Brock bit down on his lip and a crease formed between his brows. "Can I feel?"

Oh, this man was a gem. She was going to miss him when he left.

Penelope nodded and then took his hand and rested it on her stomach.

The contact of his hand on her skin had her gasping for breath. It was so intimate she hoped she didn't moan. At least not out loud.

A moment later the baby kicked right under his hand and his eyes lit up. "Oh, wow. Wow!"

"Pretty cool, huh?"

He only nodded. He kept his hand on her stomach and the baby moved against him.

"I think he knows you were important to his father."

That had broken him. Whatever she'd said in that statement caused him to retract his hand. "I should let you get dressed. Thank you for sharing this with me."

He quickly stood, walked to the door, and was gone.

Penelope lay there a moment longer thinking about how it felt to have him touch her. Even when Adam had first touched her it didn't feel the same as when Brock had laid his hand on her stomach.

It wasn't right to be lying there, in a doctor's office thinking about another man besides your late husband—especially when your husband's baby was kicking you. But Penelope couldn't help it.

Hormones, she reminded herself. She'd read about it in that book that Vivian had given her. Pregnant women were just horny. But what she wouldn't give to have Brock touch her just one more time as he had on that bed.

Penelope swung her legs over the edge of the bed and sat up. That was about the stupidest thought she'd ever had. It was time to get dressed and go on with her life.

This sad life of just her and her baby. Vivian had her girls. Amelia had Sam. And in time, she'd have her baby. It was just going to have to be enough.

Chapter Six

It should have been awkward, Brock thought as he drove back to Penelope's. He hadn't even known her a full twelve hours and yet he'd shared one of the most intimate moments of a lifetime with her.

Did he dare say Sergeant Monroe's baby was *cute*? But he was, she was. Oh, it was a confusing thought. And what about that moment when he kicked? It should have been strange to touch a woman's stomach like that, but it wasn't. In fact, it did things to him that only Shirley Ann had done when she first showed him her breasts, way back when, under the fort they'd made in his back yard. Okay, those weren't breasts and he wasn't thinking straight.

This woman with her curly blonde hair and those ocean blue eyes, and that swollen stomach—he made sure to remind himself—was toying with all those manly emotions. It had just been a long time since he'd had the pleasure of a woman. That must be it. Really, who in their right mind returns from the spoils of war and seeks out a pregnant woman for companionship?

He needed to give her the box that Sergeant Monroe had entrusted to him. He needed to high tail it out of Parson's Gulch, Oklahoma and find his way to his mother's house in Missouri. That should be far enough away to keep him sane. Yep that would do it.

And, maybe Shirley Ann was single now and looking for nothing more than a roll in the sack, because he was going to need to do something with this built up energy. Certainly the pregnant woman beside him would think he was an absolute pig for how he felt.

As they pulled up in front of the house, a man stood outside digging a hole in the yard.

"What is he doing?" Brock asked. His instinct was to jump out of the car and chase down the man ruining the grass.

He pushed back the thought. What the hell had gotten into him?

"Oh, he's putting up the sign." Her voice rose to a near squeal with anticipation. "I'm so excited. When the sign goes up, we can start taking applications for students."

She reached across the cab and grabbed his hand, still on the steering wheel. "Isn't that exciting?"

He had to admit it was. "When will you open?"

"Next month. We hope. The only thing left to do really is assemble the rooms with the tables, chairs, bookshelves, and those kinds of things. We've been getting boxes of donated toys and books. It's very exciting. Sam will pick up the play yard next weekend and we will put it up and have it inspected before we have kids here."

She clapped her hands together and bounced on the seat like a small girl.

"I'll help build the playground." The words were out before he'd even thought them.

"You will?" Those bright blue eyes opened wide and her pink lips curled up into a smile he thought he might just have to kiss.

He forced his manly cravings back down. He was a pig.

"Um, sure. If you could use the help, I'd be happy to help. I can help with the tables and the bookcases. Whatever you need."

Her brows came together. "You're heading to your mother's, in Missouri, right?"

"Yes," he said with a nod. Reality check—his mother. "I have to go see her. But I'll come right back and help."

He'd done it again! No, he would not be back. He was heading to his mother's to see her. That was where he was from. That was where he lived. He couldn't afford hotels in Oklahoma and gas back and forth. He didn't have a job. He didn't have a house. He didn't have anything. So why was he making all these promises to another man's wife after having touched her pregnant stomach after accidentally ending up in her ultrasound appointment?

"You're a man of your word, so I know you'll be back." She was smiling again and she'd called him out.

He was a man of his word. Wasn't that why he was here in the first place?

Okay, so he'd go home and see his mom. He'd call up someone and find himself a date for the night. Yep, one of those dates who didn't care if they just rolled around and did kinky things—or not. He didn't need kinky. He needed to not think of this woman—this other man's wife. Okay, that man was dead.

Damn! If it wasn't obvious, he'd bang his head on the steering wheel. Instead, he opened his door.

When she reached for her handle, he held up his hand. "I'll get it for you."

He stepped around the truck, making sure to kick the tire super hard as he passed. He reached for the handle of her door and pulled it open.

When she turned in the seat and moved to climb down, a flash of the swell of her breast from the V in her shirt nearly had him pushing her back into the truck and taking her right there. He was going to die. God was going to strike him down right there. He was going to die with a hard on.

Penelope stepped out of the truck and nearly right into Brock's arms. Was it too much to want him to wrap them around her and hold her? Oh, she wanted to be held close just one more time. But why would he want to? She was a fat, pregnant woman he didn't know.

She tucked her curls behind her ear as Brock stepped back from her. "Thank you for going. It really did mean a lot to have someone there."

"I'm glad I was there." He cleared his throat. "For Sergeant Monroe's sake. I know he'd have liked to have been there."

She wondered if he would have. In her mind, she was going to keep it as he still loved her the most. After all, she was the only wife Brock Romero had ever heard him speak of.

That should be enough to get her over this emotional bump in the road wanting men to touch her. She hadn't had another man touch her but her husband. There was no need in thinking she needed one now.

Brock moved to the side, his hand still on the door, and she stepped up onto the curb. But her footing wasn't very good and she slipped and began to tumble backward. However, she never hit the ground. A set of very sturdy, strong arms came around her right above the baby, just below her growing, swollen breasts.

She let out a horrid grunt.

"Did I hurt you? Oh, please tell me I didn't hurt the baby." Brock was scrambling to get her back on her feet and before he was done he was in front of her—arms wrapped around her.

She swallowed hard as her body pressed against his and he looked down at her with concern buried in those deep, dark eyes.

It was there. There was a moment when she was sure he felt it too—that rage of a pregnant woman's hormones and opportunity.

Her lips trembled as he looked at her. Their faces were drawing near and she was going to kiss him. Him, this man her husband sent to her whom she'd only known a day. Him, whose hands were pressed into the small of her back and lazily making circles in the fabric of her shirt. God, she was an idiot, but what did it matter if she moved in further and kissed him. He was leaving anyway.

"Mrs. Monroe!" A man called out and Penelope pushed back and out of Brock's arms. "Oh, Mrs. Monroe. I've got the sign in the truck. Would you like to see it? It's a beauty."

Penelope pushed back her shoulders and nodded to the man who had been digging the hole. "Yes. Thank you."

Brock slammed the door on the truck and the man looked back at him and gave him a genuine smile. "Nice day, huh?"

"Sure is," Brock said, but he was thinking *sure was, until you interrupted.*

He'd almost kissed her. What a shameful thing to have done.

Brock followed the man to his truck where Penelope was looking down into the truck bed. She was crying again. And there, he thought was one of the reasons not to get involved with a pregnant woman. How many times was she going to cry today?

"It's beautiful. Just beautiful."

In the truck was a wooden sign that had been carved. It read *Our Little Ones Daycare.*

"My son does the crafting. I do the lifting and the digging. He does fine work," the man said with pride in his voice. The same kind of pride his father had when he spoke of Brock.

"I can't wait until Vivian and Amelia get home. They are going to love this," Penelope smiled.

"I'll get it up for you," the man gave her a nod and extended a considerate glance at Brock.

Penelope smiled and then headed toward the house. Brock turned back to the truck to get the item he'd brought with him.

As he opened the door to the truck, he thought about Sergeant Monroe's last words as he lay bleeding to death in his arms. They were ringing clear in his head now. *We're having a baby. I'll never see that baby.* He had gasped for air and coughed up blood as he reached for his pocket and pulled out the contents. *Find her. Give her these and the box in my footlocker. Tell her I love her. Take care of her.*

Brock blinked hard against his own tears. Get the box. Give it to her. Get out of town. It would be okay if he didn't hold up to one damn promise in his life and not come back to help build the play set. Things come up all the time. He'd just tell her that's what happened.

He pulled the box from the glove compartment and shut the door. As he headed to the house, the man putting up the sign gave him a wave.

"Congratulations!" He called out and Brock turned. "Being a father is the best thing I ever did."

The man went back to digging the hole and Brock kept walking. He should have corrected the man. So why didn't he?

Penelope had left the screen open for him and he could hear noises from the kitchen. He noticed that there were flat boxes in all of the rooms. Those unassembled tables and shelves, he assumed. Guilt stabbed at him and he let out a breath. Okay, he'd be back.

She was standing over the sink with both hands on the counter and the water was running.

He set the box on the table and went to her, resting his hand on her back.

"Everything okay?"

She shook her head. "I just got hot. I needed to cool off."

That's when he noticed the hair around her face was wet and her cheeks glistened with droplets of water.

"Why don't you sit down? I'll get you some water to drink and a wet towel."

She nodded and reached for him and he helped her to the chair. Was it possible she was equally as beautiful when she didn't feel good as when she was basking in the sunlight on the front porch?

He helped her to a chair and went back to pull a cup from the cupboard and fill it with water. There were towels folded next to the sink. He took one and ran it under the cold water and that was when he heard the gasp and the sobbing cries.

Brock turned and saw her sitting over the opened box he'd brought in. A gold band was shaking between two clasped fingers.

Perhaps he should have considered what would happen when she opened that box. More tears. Of course, there were more tears. Well, he certainly couldn't leave now. Not until the others got home and could take care of her.

He set the glass of water and the towel down next to her on the table. Pulling out the chair beside her, he sat down and placed a hand on her back.

He could feel her try to push breath in and out between sobs.

"You have to calm down. This isn't good for you."

She nodded as though she knew, but couldn't stop.

"His wedding ring," she managed looking at the gold band in her hand.

"He wore it when we were in camp. He'd take it off and put it in his pocket when we were out." Brock swallowed hard. "He'd pulled it from his pocket and gave it to me before he died."

Penelope looked up at him, her eyes red and moist. "That had to have been horrible for you to hold him like that."

Now she reached her hand toward him and rested it on his.

It hadn't been on his mind—ever—that it was horrible for him. Sergeant Monroe's blood soaked his clothes. His last words rang in his ears. His wife's photos got him through the next few months. But during it all he'd been thinking about getting to her and not the emotional toll it had actually taken on him.

"He would have done the same," he said. "In fact," he cleared his throat. "He saved many lives the day he died. Mine included."

"You're here because he saved you?"

Brock nodded. "That and he sent me to you."

There were those eyes staring at him, again. Making him long to move in and take what he shouldn't.

She looked back down into the box. "These are all the pictures I sent him."

Brock nodded. "He had them in his pocket too." This was the moment he needed to come clean. "I kept them in my pocket until I landed on U.S. soil. You saved my life too."

"Me?" Her voice rose in a curious pitch and she had managed to move away from him by only leaning further back in her chair.

Brock nodded. "The anticipation of meeting you kept me going. It kept me sane in my attempt to clear my mind of what I'd seen—what I'd been through."

She relaxed a little and that, he thought, was a good sign.

"Your smile. The sparkle in your eyes. I swore sometimes I thought I could hear you laugh just as you must have been when the pictures were taken. I'd taken on the mission to find you. To return the items to you, just as Sergeant Monroe asked me to. Getting here was part of my healing—part of my forgetting."

"Wow. That's a lot of responsibility on me to make sure you're okay."

He chuckled, though she hadn't expected him to, which was obvious by the shock on her face. "I am okay. I'm very okay. I have my life. I'm back on U.S. soil. My mama will cry tears of joy and so will my father when they see me. I might have a few hard nights, but I have support." He reached for her again, because he felt he needed to touch her so she'd understand. "You let me be part of a very important day in your life. I'm only twenty-five, and I've seen a lifetime of amazing things to balance out the bad. I think I have enough support to build a solid life with."

"You came here first," she said moving in closer to him. "Why didn't you go home to your mother first?"

Simple reaction took over again and he reached up and caressed her face with his hand. "I've been looking into those eyes for months. I had to get here. I had to see them." Now he swallowed hard and felt a knot form in his stomach. "I needed to see that they didn't gaze at me the way they had been from the pictures. That gaze was for another man. A man I respected. But I think I got a little lost in it all." He hadn't realized that was the truth until he spoke it.

Her lips parted and she was near him again, just as she'd been in the street. "And these eyes," she said as she blinked them. "How do they look at you?"

How did he answer? Truthfully, he decided, because that's who he was.

"They look as though they are gazing at me."

"Hmmm," she purred. "Now what do we do about that?"

He wasn't very sure at all, but their bodies were leaning in closer and this time their lips did touch.

Was this the draw, Penelope thought? Was this why women went to bars and picked up men only to have sex with them the same night?

Her heart rate was beating so fast. Her insides were twisting. Parts of her that hadn't pulsed in nearly six months were—pulsing.

Brock's hand moved from her cheek into her hair as they deepened the kiss. Holy cow, this was one amazing trip! She couldn't believe she was six months pregnant and there was a man kissing her and making her feel like a real woman.

She could feel clouds begin to billow in her head and they spun until she thought she might just fall out of the chair.

But the moment came to a halt when someone cleared their throat and Brock pulled back from her, nearly taking a handful of her hair as well.

He was on his feet and when she could focus she saw Vivian standing in the doorway, the girls giggling and tucked behind her.

Penelope struggled to clear her mind, but everything was still spinning. Oh, why had she had to interrupt?

"Sorry, ma'am. We were—I just…" He stopped, pushed his shoulders back and looked Vivian in the eye. "I'm very sorry."

"Girls, why don't you go out to the front and get the iPad out of my bag and watch a movie?" The girls scurried off laughing. But Vivian wasn't laughing. She stepped further into the kitchen with her hands fisted on her hips. "Do the two of you mind telling me what's going on?"

"I got caught up," Penelope spurted out. "I'm all stirred up and crazy right now with this body." She planted her hands on her stomach. "When Brock touched my stomach today at the doctor's office I got all giddy."

She saw him fight off the smile that was trying to form when Vivian took another step toward them. "You took him with you?" She turned to Brock. "You went with her? You went *in* with her?"

"Yes, ma'am. I offered to accompany her, but my going in, well that was a misunderstanding. But I must say, it was an experience I will never forget."

Penelope felt the tension drain from her body. He had thought the experience was as special as she had. Would Adam have even been that enthused?

"Oh," Vivian said and then sat down in the chair that Brock had occupied. "I'm sorry I wasn't there."

Penelope had been too, but she was fairly sure she'd gotten over that.

"I think it's time for me to head out," Brock said and Penelope stood, slowly.

"You're heading to your parents?"

"Yes. It's time they know I'm here." He took her hands in his. "Thank you for sharing your day with me."

"Thank you for going."

"My offer still stands to come and help with the play yard."

"Right, I, um," she looked down at Vivian. "I think that would be nice."

"I'll talk to you in a few days."

Vivian planted her hands flat on the table. "Oh for heaven's sake go ahead and kiss her goodbye. Don't let me be so shocked by it all that you keep falling over yourselves."

Penelope waited as Brock leaned in and pressed another kiss to her lips. It was quick, but it still drove her just as wild.

He gave her a smile and finally turned and walked out.

Penelope sighed and Vivian moaned.

"Seriously? Some guy shows up here and says he knew Adam, now you're kissing him? What is wrong with you?"

"I'm sorry." she fell back into her chair. "I couldn't help myself. I have all these hormones chugging through my body and I don't have an outlet."

"So you think he's it?"

"I just happen to think he's very kind and compassionate."

Vivian nodded. "What's all of this?" She pulled the box toward her.

"This is what Adam sent with him. This is why he's here—to give me this."

Vivian flipped through the pictures of Penelope. "Who took these?"

Penelope bit down on her lip. "Adam. When I got them printed off, I sent them to him. That's when I told him about the baby."

She could see the change in Vivian when she looked at the pictures. It must have been hard to even be cordial to her when everything Penelope said or did only reinstated that her husband had been unfaithful to her.

Vivian put the pictures back in the box and looked inside again.

"What in the hell?" She pulled out a pocket watch and dangled it by the chain. "Where did you get this? Where did Brock get this?"

Penelope stared at her. Her face had flushed and her brows narrowed.

"I didn't know it was in there. I hadn't looked all the way," Penelope stammered as she watched Vivian examine the watch.

"Son-of-a-bitch!" She opened the front and looked at it again. "He had this the whole time?"

"What is it?"

"It's his grandfather's pocket watch. The one his mother accused me of stealing and selling."

Penelope wasn't completely sure what had happened between Vivian and Adam's mother, but she was sure it was about to get even more interesting.

Chapter Seven

Watching Vivian process the moment was a bit like watching a chameleon change its colors, Penelope thought. Her face had become bright red when she saw the pocket watch and then pale white as she held it in her hand. Her hands began to shake and then she bit down and Penelope could hear her grind her teeth.

"Why did his mother accuse you of stealing it?" Penelope asked.

"Because she's a hag," she said in a near whisper looking down the hall toward where the girls were sitting. "She accused me of stealing this very watch and selling it. And don't you think it's odd that Brock said Adam never got any letters from me? That damn footlocker should have been plastered with pictures of his daughters. I sent him new pictures nearly every week. I just assumed he didn't care."

"You think she had something to do with that?"

"Damn straight I do. You saw how upset she got over everything. His father was always escorting her out of situations."

"Then why did you spend so much time around her?"

Vivian gave a low growl. "I wanted her to accept me. She loved him. She loved my girls. I just wanted her to want me too."

Penelope reached for her. "She's out of the picture now. You don't have to worry about her."

That caused Vivian to let out a sarcastic snort. "Is that what you think? Don't be so naive. This is her grandchild," she said resting her hand on Penelope's stomach. "So are they." She pointed down the hall. "They are all she has left of him."

Penelope felt that panic that had her breaking out in a sweat that came with pure fear. "Do you think she'll come after my baby?" She rested her hands on her stomach.

"No. And don't you go freaking out on me. I just think you need to watch your step. Especially with that Brock guy."

"Brock? Why?"

"Some guy shows up with items I've spent nearly six years looking for and stories of how wonderful Adam was? Maybe she sent him. Did you consider that? How do we know he was with Adam? His parents were told how he died. Maybe that's his story too."

No, she didn't want to think that. But, what if?

"He's coming back next week," Penelope said softly, hoping Vivian wouldn't become even angrier with her. "He's offered to help put the play yard together and the classroom furniture."

Again, Vivian let out a groan. "There is only one reason I'm going to agree to that. We sure could use the help. Besides," she said cupping the watch in her hand. "We could use a little more muscle and he had plenty." She finally smiled. "And it wouldn't hurt to have him close by. If he is working with Adam's mother against us, it would be my pleasure to hang him by his balls."

Penelope gasped and covered her mouth, but Vivian hadn't seemed to notice. Just the thought of harming Brock seemed to give her some sense of calm.

Penelope wasn't sure that was what she wanted for him. Maybe she should warn him.

~*~

Gwendolyn Romero hadn't disappointed Brock. When she'd come to the door and saw him she'd nearly gone into hysterics.

It had taken her another three minutes before she was calm enough to even open the door to him. When she did, he pulled her into him and just held her.

She'd caused enough commotion that his father had come looking to see what was going on.

When he saw Brock standing there holding her, his father wrapped his arms around both of them. And there they stood in the doorway of his childhood home, sobbing and hugging.

Brock wasn't sure how long they'd stood there in the doorway holding each other. Some part of him expected his sister and her family to show up and his brother and his wife. Hadn't everyone in Missouri heard his mother?

They'd gone straight back into the kitchen because she'd calmed down enough now and she wanted to feed him. He wasn't going to argue. It had been a very long time since he'd had a decent meal—a very long time. And though his mother's cooking was anything but decent, he'd missed it.

He sat down at the table as his mother fluttered around the kitchen. His father sat across from him.

Brock thought he looked healthy, which was a bonus. When Brock had enlisted, his father was taking insulin for diabetes. Now, he looked as though he'd lost about forty pounds and there was a healthy glow to him. That pleased Brock. The thought of his dad being sick hadn't helped while he was dealing with his injuries and the vivid realities of war and death.

Gregory Romero had done his share of active duty. He too had a few scars to prove it.

"It's good to see you," his father said as he rested his arms on the table.

"Thank you. I can't tell you how happy I am to be home."

"You don't have to," his father said on a laugh. "I'll never forget that final trip. Nothing like it."

"I'll agree."

His father leaned in while his mother clinked plates and pots around as she mumbled to herself as she did when she cooked.

"How's your injury?" his father asked in a hushed tone.

"It's all healed. I'm fine."

His father nodded slowly. "Your dreams? How's your sleep? Are you doing okay?"

Brock knew where he was going with this. "Do you still have that beer fridge in the garage?"

A smile formed on his father's lips. "You haven't seen what your brother and I did to the garage. C'mon." He stood and turned to Brock's mother. "I'm taking him out to show him the cave."

She nodded and kept moving about. Brock wasn't sure if he was going to have a complete feast or if he'd come back to a sandwich and chips. His mother wasn't the best cook—at all—but she sure enjoyed trying.

Brock's father escorted him through the adjoining door and out to the garage. It wasn't the garage Brock had remembered. This looked more like one of those garage take over shows where they come in and make it the ultimate "Man Cave."

"Holy cow!" Brock laughed when he saw the old 50's diner themed table in the corner and the enormous flat screen TV on the wall. "Do you even park in here anymore?"

"No," his father let out a snort. "I'm afraid to mess up this floor."

Brock looked down at the tiled floor done in a black and white checkered pattern. "This has to be one of the coolest garages ever."

"Mason and I think so."

His father walked toward the full sized refrigerator in the corner and pulled out two beers. He handed one to Brock and he twisted off the top.

He took a long pull and let it roll on his tongue. "I have to say that has to be the best beer I have ever had."

His father smiled and tapped the neck of his beer bottle to Brock's. "I remember it well. C'mon, let's sit."

His father led him to the table, picked up the remote, and clicked on a random sports channel.

"How are Mason and Sadie?" Brock asked about his siblings, though he'd had emails from both of them before he'd headed back to America.

"Mason is keeping busy with that little business of his."

"Little? He showed me a picture of his setup. I think he's doing better than keeping busy."

"I don't think you can make a living and raise a family testing video games for companies."

Brock laughed as he pulled again from his beer. He didn't want to discredit his father's thinking, but he was pretty sure Mason was doing just that.

"Wait, you said family. Are him and Chelsea…"

"Expecting?" His father smiled wider. "Maybe he didn't want you to know."

He doubted that. His brother told him *everything*.

"Maybe." He nodded. "That's exciting. Must be something in the water."

His father's brows drew together. "Why do you say that?"

"Nothing, Dad." He laughed again. "I just have a friend who's expecting too. Don't get too worried. I had nothing to do with it."

"Well, that's why I think he needs a real job."

"I'm sure if he needs one, he'll get one." He took another sip from his beer. "Sadie said the kids grew nearly two inches since I've seen them last. I'll have to stop by."

"I think your mother would like to have everyone over for dinner since you're back. Can you make time for that?"

Brock gave it some thought. "Yeah. I have some things I promised to do, but I'm sure I can do it whenever Mom wants to."

His father grew quiet and rolled the beer bottle between his palms.

"You're okay though? I mean you've healed? How is your sleep? You're not drinking are you?" He looked at the bottle. "I mean excessively."

Brock reached across the small table and rested his hand on his father's. "I'm fine. The bullet left me with a scar." He pulled up his sleeve and showed him his shoulder. "I was very lucky. I know that. As for what I saw and what I went through," he considered. "I know I'll have some restless nights. I might even look into some support groups. I'm not above looking for help if I need it."

His father nodded. "You always did have a good head on your shoulders." He sat back and took a pull from his beer. "So now what? Now that you're home, what are your plans?"

Brock sipped his beer and let out a breath. "I'm going to head to Parson's Gulch, Oklahoma for a bit. Sergeant Monroe's family is opening a daycare center in his grandmother's old house in town. They've done a lot of work to it. I offered to go down and help with assembling the play yard and the classrooms."

His father narrowed his eyes on him. "There's more. What else is there?"

Brock couldn't help but smile. Just the thought of Penelope made him do that. "Okay, there's a girl. Nothing big," he tried to be calm and use his words carefully. "I just met her. She's got a lot on her plate now. But, she's good people."

His father crossed his arms over his chest and nodded. "You have a way of reading people. If you say she's good people, she is."

That meant a lot coming from his father. Now, to convince his mother would be a different story.

Chapter Eight

Penelope sat at the table in the small kitchen of the old house with Amelia and Vivian pouring over the photos Vivian had taken of her wrecked home.

"I hardly filled up Sam's truck. The tree had fallen in before they got to it and everything was ruined," Vivian said.

Penelope looked at the pictures from the girls' room and it brought her to tears. She'd only had a few very precious toys when she was young. Toys her mother deemed educational and useful, but she would have been devastated to lose them.

"I wish we could do something to replace it all," Penelope scanned through the photos again.

"I've lived in this town my whole life. I've seen it leveled worse than this. I was unlucky this time, but my girls and I were safe. I can't even be upset about all of this."

"I still don't know what you were doing here. It was like a divine intervention that you weren't at the house," Amelia said, looking over Penelope's shoulder.

Penelope looked up at Vivian, who was already smiling wide. Then Sam cleared his throat.

"I think the two of you need to come clean and tell her about the body you were burying in the basement that night."

Penelope nearly broke out in a laugh when Amelia gave him a shake of her head.

"Did Adam's mother make an appearance that night?" she asked, looking right in Vivian's direction.

Vivian's humored look sobered up. "You say crap like that as if you think I'd do that."

"Oh, lighten up. I was kidding."

Sam rested a hand on Vivian's shoulder. "I carried an enormous box down there today," he stressed his words. "Maybe you should take a walk."

Penelope clapped. "Oh, goodie! It came." She stood from her chair nearly knocking Amelia back.

"What is going on?"

Vivian walked past her and opened the basement door. "Shut up and come see where your grave is."

"*My* grave? You'd rather bury me in the basement than Adam's mother?"

"Oh, you two." Penelope stepped between them. "Will you ever stop?"

It frustrated her when they went at each other. Though sometimes she couldn't tell if they were fighting or messing with her.

She reached for the switch to turn on the light for the staircase and then took her first carefully coordinated step.

Going down the stairs had already become a balancing act with her body.

Penelope cleared the last step and could hear the girls barreling toward her. How Amelia had no idea what was down here was beyond her. Those girls had been so excited she was sure they'd never get the last piece there before Amelia knew what they were hiding.

She looked up the steps and Sam walked in front of Amelia as if to shield her.

"C'mon. Let me down there," she scolded.

"You'll get there," he argued back.

Vivian stood at the bottom of the steps looking up at Amelia. "I don't plan on always being nice to you."

"Obviously," Amelia retorted.

"But, you've selflessly made changes in your life to keep my family intact and to take care of Penelope and her baby.

We can't repay you for that. You didn't have to leave us with anything. You could have walked away."

"I never would have done that."

"I know that now," Vivian said, her voice soft and sincere. "You only ever asked for one thing."

She stepped aside and stood with Penelope and the girls as Amelia turned the corner and saw what had been planned out just for her.

"Oh! You built me a gym." Her voice rose in pitch as her eyes grew wider and brighter as she took in the sight of barbells, dumbbells, and big rubber balls.

"It was the least we could do for you," Penelope added.

"This is great." She moved toward the heavy bag. "I've needed to punch something." She let loose a punch into the bag.

"Yes, you've been doing that in your sleep," Sam joked.

Amelia narrowed a stare at him and then quickly looked around again. "You all put down a sparring mat. Who wants me to take them down first?"

Penelope wondered why she'd turned and looked right at her. But a moment later the girls were right by her side punching and kicking the bag with laughter.

"I guess I should have bought them one of those years ago," Vivian said. "I could have used it too. I certainly would have liked to kick the crap out of a few people. This would have vented that better than me holding it in."

"Now you can come down here and let it out," Penelope gave her a smile.

Sam leaned up against the basement wall and crossed his arms over his chest. "I guess other than assembling the furniture, the last item we have to address—now that this is done—is the attic. We're going to need storage space and maybe extra office space, even if we keep the room across from Penelope's as an office."

"Are you sure you want to go up there?" Amelia laughed as she landed a roundhouse kick into the pad and the girls giggled. "Remember last time you tried to open the door." She grinned. "It knocked you on your ass."

Sam rubbed his chest where the set of stairs had come down and hit him. "Oh, I remember. That's why you're going up first."

Amelia gave him a wink. "That's why I love my man."

Penelope rested her hands on her stomach as the baby kicked. "I'm beginning to wonder if this kid is going to take after Amelia. I've done some reading and I don't think he should be kicking quite this hard yet."

Emma hurried over to her. "Is it a boy?"

"I don't know. I just use the terms loosely. Tomorrow I might say her."

"I want a sister," Ava added.

"You have a sister, goober," Emma retorted as Penelope rubbed her stomach again. "Can I feel?"

Penelope nodded and took Emma's hand and rested it where the baby had kicked. "I don't know if he'll…"

"Wow!" Emma's eyes grew wide. "I felt that."

"Me. Me." Ava held out her hand.

Penelope placed it on her stomach and held it flat. Ava's face crinkled up as if she were concentrating hard to make the baby move.

"Where is he?" she asked.

"Well honey, maybe he went back to sleep."

"Does he have a bedroom in there?"

Penelope laughed. "Sorta."

"And pillows?"

"No. I'm his pillow. He's just in there." The baby kicked again. "Oh, there. He's trying to get comfy. Did you feel that?"

Ava pulled back her hand. "Ewww."

That caused everyone to laugh and when Penelope looked up toward Vivian, even her eyes held humor. That eased Penelope's heart. She loved Vivian's girls and they were excited that the baby would be their baby sister or brother. She wanted to keep that enthusiasm.

When they all made it back to the kitchen, Vivian began to pick up the iPad and store it in her bag. "It looks like they'll start the demo on the house next week."

"Will you rebuild there?" Penelope asked.

"I don't know. I never liked it out there anyway. I have a choice now," she said softly. "I can have what I want. Live where I want. Have a front door that works—if I want."

Penelope couldn't believe the same man she'd married was the one who had married Vivian and all, but forgot her in the small run down house on the edge of town.

"Would anyone like to see the picture I got today?" Penelope said softly as everyone gathered their things.

"Picture?" Amelia hoisted her bag over her shoulder.

"Of the baby."

Amelia and Vivian exchanged looks.

Vivian's shoulders dropped. "We really let you down."

"It's okay. Really." Penelope pulled the picture out of her bag on the table. "Here."

She handed Vivian the picture and Amelia and Sam looked over her shoulder.

"These never cease to amaze me," Vivian said softly. "Look at his little nose and fingers."

"I think it looks like a girl," Amelia added.

Sam snorted out a laugh. "I can't tell anything."

"Penelope, he's gorgeous. And he's healthy?" Vivian looked up and asked.

Penelope nodded. "He's doing great. No concerns."

Amelia moved to her and gave her a hug. "I'll be there for the next one, okay?"

Penelope nodded and Sam moved in and kissed her on the cheek. "I'll try not to pull her away." Penelope smiled and Sam leaned into her ear. "I bought more of those candies you like too, for the board room." He kissed her cheek again and left with his arm around Amelia.

Penelope could feel her face flush. He did know she'd been eating all the snacks.

"I guess I should get the girls home." Vivian handed her back the picture after gazing at it one more time. "You'll be okay here?"

"This is my home now."

"I'm a phone call away if you need me." She hugged Penelope and then gathered the girls and they walked out of the house.

Penelope sat at the table and thought for a moment. What would people really think if they knew why and how these women were thrust into each other's lives?

She rubbed her stomach and looked down at her ankles that were swelling and could use an ice pack and some elevation.

The thought became crystal clear though. She'd been mildly upset that they weren't there with her for her ultrasound. After all, they were all she had now. But never, from the moment she'd found out she was pregnant, had she considered Adam's role in her child's life. That was odd, wasn't it? When she'd dream about the baby, she didn't dream of Adam there at all.

Was that a sign? Did it mean anything really?

Then she thought about Brock.

He'd manned up and been there for her. Had he wanted to be? Even when he could have turned around and left the room, he hadn't.

The baby responded to his touch—to his voice. She'd responded too, hadn't she?

She pressed her fingers to her lips. It was more than just circumstance, right? She'd felt something. Had he felt it too?

Penelope turned off the lights in the kitchen and checked all the doors before heading upstairs to her room with her phone and the baby's picture.

Locking the bedroom door, because it just made her feel safer, she turned on the lights and hit the button on the television which sat on the dresser. An old *Andy Griffith Show* rerun was on. That would be just calm enough for her brain, she thought. A little trip to Mayberry.

As Opie told his dad something, Barney added his wit—then Aunt Bea added her wisdom. All the while Penelope readied herself for bed.

After dressing, she plopped down on her bed, her hands firmly on her stomach. Her cell phone and the picture bounced, grasping her attention.

What would Brock think if she sent him the picture? Would it freak him out and send him running? Would he find it charming and sentimental? A token of their day together?

After a few moments deliberation, she decided to just send it. The worse that would happen would be he'd never return her text or return at all. A few kisses lost would be it—or so she was trying hard to convince herself.

She snapped the picture, scrolled through her contacts, and sent it with the message, *we would like to thank you for being there today. Penelope and Baby.*

Promptly, she silenced the phone and set it on the nightstand upside-down. She needed rest. The last thing she needed to do was continually check the phone all night waiting for his reply.

Chapter Nine

Long talks with his sister had always been one of Brock's favorite things. She was only four years older, but she'd been wise since infancy.

Sadie had a calm about her, which usually made everyone around her open up. Brock was no different. There was never a secret he could keep or a feeling he could hide from her. He supposed that was what made her such a wonderful mother.

"I think you look really skinny," she said as she rocked her two-year-old on her lap on the back porch. He'd fallen asleep as it was already past ten o'clock. The other two were inside sleeping on couches and her husband in a recliner.

"I'm fine. Desert heat will do that to you."

She nodded and clucked her tongue. "Getting shot will do that too. Is your shoulder okay?"

"It's fine. I'm fine. I'm happy to be home."

"We're glad you're back too. There were a lot of restless nights in many homes you know."

He nodded. He knew. "I promised Dad I'd get help if I needed it. But I promise you, I'm okay."

Sadie kissed her son's hair. His blond curls were growing damp with sweat, but she didn't seem to mind that pressed against her.

"Are you going to find a place or stay here? We have a room over the garage you know."

He smiled. They all looked out for him. "Actually, I'm going to head to Oklahoma in a few days. I made a promise to a friend that I'd look after someone and help her out. And then I promised her I'd be back."

Even on the dark, only moonlit porch, he could see the spark in his sister's eyes. "She."

"Yes. Sergeant Monroe's wife needs some help getting her business going. I offered to help her out."

Sadie's foot kept pushing the rocker in a slow, steady rhythm that kept him as calm as the boy in her arms.

"What kind of business?"

"A daycare center. They've refurbished an old house. All that is left is to put the play yard and the tables and chairs together."

"That's a wonderful venture," she smiled and he could see the glow of her white teeth. "I have six boxes of young reader books in my garage. Do you think she'd like them?"

And that, he thought, was just like his sister. She'd given her teaching career a break to be a mother. And because it was Sadie, she wouldn't think a thing about giving her collection to someone she didn't know if it meant someone would benefit.

"I think they would appreciate that."

"They? Not just she?"

Brock ran his fingers through his hair and sucked in a deep breath. "It seems as though Sergeant Monroe had a few wives."

"As in he divorced often?"

"As in he just kept marrying women. Only they didn't know it."

Sadie's foot grew still and the night crept in around them. "A bigamist?"

Brock nodded. "Penelope, the wife he sent me to take care of, only found out about the other wives when he died."

"That's horrible."

He rested his hands on his thighs. "That wasn't the man I knew. Not the man who saved me."

"Some men can hide secrets."

"He did quite a job." Brock let himself relax and began to rock his chair. "They are opening this business together so that the kids can be taken care of. But it's a funny thing, you'd have thought they were all sisters they way they look out for each other."

"Trauma can make for some strong allies even if they aren't ones you thought you'd have."

Didn't he know that?

"No matter what, they'll take care of each other."

He heard her hum and that meant she was thinking. "You've already met this woman?"

"Yes."

"Before you were discharged?"

And he'd been caught. "No."

She let out another hum. "You went there first?"

Brock leaned his arms on his legs and moved toward his sister. "Don't you dare tell her."

"She'd be hurt that you didn't come home first."

And didn't he know that too? "I needed to fulfill a promise to the man who saved my life."

The pace of Sadie's rocking picked up. "Moving in on his wife isn't fulfilling a promise."

Fire began to burn in his belly. That wasn't the way of it and he couldn't believe his own sister said that. But before he even could comment he thought about how it would look. And that was exactly what he would have thought too, if it were anyone else.

"She met him and married him two weeks later. He was deployed and then he died. She didn't really know him."

"And you're a good replacement?"

Brock grit his teeth, trying to remind himself he didn't want this conversation to become any louder and he didn't want to wake the sweet boy in his sister's arms.

"I carried her picture with me for nearly three months. She saved me as much as her husband did. I needed to go to her. I needed to give her what Sergeant Monroe had given me to give to her. I had to fulfill a promise."

"And then you fell in love with her."

Was it some kind of psychic power his sister had? He wouldn't have said he'd fallen in love with Penelope Monroe, but what did you say about a person who had consumed you for months and then invited you into her life the day you met her? And he'd felt the spark when they kissed. He would be surprised if everyone hadn't felt the earth move. He sure had.

And then there was the baby. Did he have a connection to the baby? After all, when he touched her the baby moved as if he were reacting to Brock's touch.

Maybe he did need some help. Yes, he'd look into that. It was impossible to fall in love with someone in one day. Men didn't do that. Okay, Sadie had done that. And his parents had done that. Ah! Mason had known his wife for eight years before they married. See! It wasn't always possible.

"I'm not in love with her. I'm interested, but let's face it. She has a lot on her plate."

"She's mourning her husband."

Was that really true? "There's more to it than that."

"What?"

Brock pulled his phone from his pocket and pulled up the text message Penelope had sent him an hour ago. He handed his phone to his sister who skillfully held it with the hand tucked under her son's head.

"Are you kidding me? She's pregnant?"

"Six months."

"Brock," she scolded.

"I know. I know," he said taking the phone back and looking at the picture. "I want to be there for her and the baby. I feel it is the right thing to do. She needs a friend."

"You said she had that."

"She needs another one," he argued.

"I guess you don't need the room over the garage. It looks like you're moving to Oklahoma."

He hadn't thought about it that way, but if it all worked out—yes, he was moving.

"I'll come by for those books tomorrow."

Sadie let out a small laugh. "I want to come to the baby shower. And don't you go marrying her without your family there."

Brock smiled in the dark and looked down at the picture. That was a thought for the future—far in the future. For now he wanted to show up with boxes of books, ready to build play yards.

He traced his finger over the image of the baby. It wouldn't be so bad to be there for the baby when he needed him. Even young boys needed a male figure—father or not.

If the baby was a girl, that'd be okay too. Girls needed someone to take them to father/daughter dances and to ward off would be boyfriends.

Brock swallowed hard as his sister rose with her son in her arms. What was he thinking? He didn't know this woman. He certainly didn't need a baby right now, so why was he thinking like that?

However, he could certainly use a friend and he knew she could too. Tomorrow he'd set out for Oklahoma with the mindset of friendship. And if he could keep his lips and hands off of her then, he'd consider it a success.

Chapter Ten

It was nearly three o'clock when Brock arrived in front of *Our Little Ones Daycare*. He didn't see the Mustang, but it certainly didn't mean she wasn't home.

As he stepped out of his truck, he could hear laughter from the back yard. He was sure that in time that would be the only sound he'd hear coming from the house.

From the truck, he pulled out a bouquet of flowers he'd picked up on his way into town. What woman wouldn't want flowers?

Later he'd bring in the boxes of books from his sister's house. But for now, he'd just say hello and feel things out.

As of last night, when he'd rested his head on the pillow in his old bedroom, he'd had some clarity. What if Penelope was upset over the kisses they'd shared? What if she'd been caught up in the moment and really didn't feel that way about him?

After all, he had an advantage over her. He knew all about her. He'd seen her every day for months. But to her—he was a stranger.

When he reached the door, he rang the bell and waited. He truly hoped it would be Penelope who would answer.

However, when the door opened he smiled hoping to ease any earlier tension, but the look on Vivian Monroe's face did not say *I'm glad to see you.*

She fisted her hands on her hips and glared at him from behind the screen.

"I really didn't think we'd see you again."

Brock bit down on the inside of his cheek. "I told Penelope I'd be back to help. I'd really like to lend a hand."

"And you're standing there holding flowers because you came to help with the play yard?"

"Ma'am, I'm sorry if I've done anything to upset you. I…"

"I said you didn't have to call me ma'am," she said moving toward the door handle.

"I certainly do if I've offended you in some way. I feel as though you think I'm a threat."

Vivian cautiously looked behind her as if checking on the girls by sound before she stepped out of the house, closing the door behind her.

"I'm going to be frank. I find a lot of sketchiness to your story."

"My story?" He tried to relax his shoulders when he realized he was standing defensively.

"You show up out of nowhere with this story that Adam sent you. You have pictures of Penelope and an item which I've been searching for, for years."

"I don't understand."

"That box you brought. You had his grandfather's pocket watch in it. How did you get that? Where did you get those pictures? And where do you get off telling her that you never knew he was married until he married her? The man was married to me for ten years and has two beautiful daughters."

"I swear to you, I didn't know about his girls—or you. And I'm only here because Sergeant Monroe sent me."

Her eyes narrowed. "I don't like that you've got her all twisted up. She didn't know Adam at all, really. And now here you are with stories about him and gifts. Why don't you come clean? What does his mother want?"

Now he was just confused. What was this woman talking about? Why was she accusing him? This wasn't what he signed on for—and what business was it of hers anyway? Sergeant Monroe had sent him. He'd asked him to fulfill a dying wish and he'd done so. It just so happened that he was immensely attracted to Sergeant Monroe's wife—the younger one because the one in front of him was just damn scary. But if anyone was going to kick him off the porch of the house, it was going to be Penelope.

"I've never met Sergeant Monroe's mother. The only contact I've had with her was when I called to find Mrs. Monroe," he reminded himself he'd have to be more specific with that phrase. "Penelope."

"She just sent you on over?"

"No."

That had Vivian shifting her weight, which meant he'd surprised her.

"His mother went into hysterics when I called. I mentioned that I was looking for his wife. And then specifically for Penelope. The woman screamed and cried. I have no idea what she was going on about. And then his father calmly took the phone and directed me here."

Her shoulders softened. "That would make more sense. He's a very calm man and I don't know how he does it."

Brock smiled. "I do remember Sergeant Monroe making a comment once about his mother being the most high-strung woman he'd ever known."

"For once, I couldn't agree with him more." She clasped her hands in front of her and wrung them. "I'm not comfortable with you moving in on Penelope and getting her all worked up though. I was more than a little surprised to find you kissing in the kitchen."

Okay, he had that one coming. His mother would say the same thing if she'd seen them. But this wasn't Penelope's mother.

"I understand," he said. "Perhaps we were a bit irrational."

She shrugged. "Well, all I'm asking is that you be mindful of her. She jumped into marriage. She's pregnant and widowed. I don't want her hurt."

He wasn't sure why it surprised him that a woman in Vivian Monroe's position would care about someone like Penelope. She should have been a threat and Vivian should have had the same reaction as Sergeant Monroe's mother had. "Ma'am, I'd never hurt her. I can promise you that. Swear it even."

She was studying him. Eventually, her eyes lightened and he knew that she'd come to peace with him.

"She's at work right now. She's not even here."

Brock nodded. "I came to help out here. That was my promise. And I brought some items for your classrooms," he added. "My sister was a teacher before she had kids. She sent her classroom books for you if you'd like them."

For a moment, he thought her eyes might have misted over. Then, a smile formed on her lips. "I think that is very sweet. We'd love them."

"I'll get them from the truck."

She nodded. "Before you leave I'd like you to give me her address so I can send her a card. That is more than generous of someone to do that."

Now he smiled wide. "It's just how my family works," he said with pride. A statement was never truer than that one. If his mother, father, and brother knew what he was up to—they'd be there too. Maybe if he found they needed it, he'd call his dad and brother and have them come down. His father was a genius with a saw and wood. And by the looks of his father's garage, his brother wasn't too shabby at designing either. He turned toward the car to get the books. It might just work in his favor that Penelope wasn't home. If he could win Vivian over, things were looking up.

~*~

The look on Sam's face was priceless, Penelope thought, but her own embarrassment had her face flushed with heat. In front of her were no less than sixteen mini candy bar wrappers.

"Don't grin at me like that," she said with her mouth full.

"I can't help it. You're cute." He moved to her and wiped his thumb over her chin. "You had a little right there."

Penelope swallowed hard. "Why do you keep buying these? I'm going to gain sixty pounds."

"You'll probably get diabetes too."

She slumped in her chair. "Can we do something different for the snacks in there? Your clients don't even eat them."

"Honey, how can they? They're all out here on your desk." He laughed. She sulked.

It was true though. She was going to be sick and fat. She didn't want that.

Penelope leaned back in her chair and rested her hands on her growing stomach. "What are you going to do when I leave?" she asked. Both of them knew this was a temporary job. When the baby was born, she'd go to the daycare to work. That had been the plan.

His grin diminished. "My mother has already told me she'll be back."

"That's good."

Sam shrugged. "She's a great help, I won't lie. It'll be nice to have her here until I hire a replacement. But she's already driving Amelia crazy with wedding ideas. I don't think Amelia is humored by it. She wants a small and very simple wedding."

"I know. I've tried to ask her about details and she just shuts me up. She doesn't want to over think it." She rubbed her stomach. "At least no matter what she chooses, by New Year's Eve I can wear a regular dress.

Sam smiled. She knew it wasn't the thought of her wearing a normal dress. He was thinking about New Year's Eve. She could see it sparkle in his eyes.

The thought made her a little sad, so she gathered the candy wrappers and threw them into the trash can under her desk.

Adam had gazed at her, made her swoon. But looking at Sam, just thinking of Amelia, she was sure no one had ever thought of her like that.

Though, she thought again as Sam retreated to his office, the other night in the street when she'd tripped and Brock had caught her, he'd looked at her like that.

Those dark eyes had become darker—intensified by the dark lashes that hooded them. Was that the look? Was that sparkle in Sam's eyes the same as the shimmer that had been in Brock's?

The ringing of the phone snapped her out of her delusion.

An hour later, Penelope was in Adam's Mustang headed back to the old house on Main Street. The town was looking normal, she thought. The broken trees, which had been blown over in the tornado, had been cut away. The windows in houses had been fixed. There weren't as many men hanging from electric and telephone poles now either. Everything was healing.

She hadn't driven out to where Vivian's house was. She wasn't sure her heart could handle it. In less than a moment, everything had been lost. All she could do was continue to pray and thank God they hadn't been home. They'd been at the old house on Main arranging the basement for Amelia to have a gym. After all, it was all she'd asked for and they owed her so much more.

Vivian would probably never say that aloud, but Penelope sure would make it a point to let her know how much she appreciated her giving up everything just to help them out. She could have walked away with everything, but she hadn't.

As she turned down Main Street, she could already see the sign in front of the daycare. It was beautiful. The sun reflected off the new window. The grass was plush and green, because Sam kept it that way. And the street had a truck on it, which made her heart rate kick up.

Brock was there.

Instantly her palms grew damp. He'd come. He'd actually come to help.

As she parked the car she tried to ignore the flutters in her stomach, which weren't the baby moving. Truly he was a man of his word.

A quick check in the mirror and she decided she looked as good as she possibly could. And just as quickly, as she maneuvered her body from the car, she remembered there was more to her than a pretty face. A man might like a pretty woman, but one with a bowling ball shoved under her shirt—that was another thing.

Either way, she wanted to see him. Was he there just because he said he'd be? Or maybe—just maybe—did he come back because of her?

She stopped at the end of the walk and looked up at the house. She took a deep breath and tried to clear her mind. Certainly her thoughts were being run on desperation. That had to stop. She couldn't just want to be with a man because he said nice things or fulfilled a few promises. Adam had done that. Resting her hands on her stomach, she willed herself to calm.

Brock Romero was just a nice guy. She had to remember that. He wasn't there to sweep her pregnant self off her feet. There was no fairy tale here. This was reality. She was a widowed single mother and that was what she'd always be.

He was the man who held her husband when he died and was making good on a promise. In a week he'd go back home and she'd grow bigger. This was how it was and she knew that well enough.

But, for a moment she'd put on a smile, cordially welcome him, and cry herself to sleep when she went to bed.

As she climbed the front steps, she could hear whistling. Was that *Zippity-Do-Dah*? Instantly, a smile formed on her lips. She turned the knob to the front door. Oh, thank the Lord, the air conditioner had been fixed and turned on. She was going to have to kiss someone's feet for that.

Of course, the cool air didn't do much once she saw him and her body heat began to rise. He was seated on the floor with a small yellow chair between his outstretched legs. He had on a baseball cap turned backward, and he was assembling what looked like his hundredth chair.

The whistle stopped on *what a wonderful day* and he looked up as if he'd sensed her. The corner of his mouth turned up into a smile and a dimple deepened in his cheek.

Okay, she just might faint right there. He was the heat in the room and she was burning.

"Hey," he said with a nod of his head. "I'd get up, but I think my legs are numb."

She looked around the room. Chairs and tables, in mini size, and a bookcase had been assembled. "You did all of this today?"

"Yeah. I haven't even scratched the surface. You guys have a lot of stuff for a few rooms. But I think the kids are going to be comfy." He pushed the small yellow chair back and rolled to his knees. He stayed there for a moment before rising and immediately reaching for his left shoulder.

When he winced, Penelope moved toward him. "Are you okay?"

"Scar tissue," he said as he rolled his shoulder. "It tightens up."

She licked her lips as she moved toward him. "Scar tissue? What happened?"

"Bullet."

Her hand rose as she neared him and moved right to his T-shirt sleeve. "Can I see?"

"Hold on," he said as he lifted off his shirt.

Penelope held down the sigh that so wanted to escape as he revealed what was under that shirt. A tight stomach. Sculpted shoulders and chest. He had a tattoo on his side—the U.S. flag. But marring the fine surface of the man's skin was the raised red scar only inches from where one would hold their hand over their heart.

Her knees were weak, but she fought to stand.

Her hand lifted, as though of its own will, to touch the scar. "This is what happened when Adam saved you?" Her voice cracked when she'd said his name.

"Yeah. Couple more inches and..."

Quickly, she retracted her hand. It was too much to think about.

"You two need to get a room if you're going to be kissing and undressing all the time," Vivian's voice rang through the room.

Anger snapped in Penelope and she spun toward her. "He was showing me where he was shot. Right above his heart. This is a man Adam saved before his life was ended.

You could show him some respect and stop being so bitchy."

The words flew from her mouth and just as quickly she wanted to retract them when she saw the look of shock on Vivian's face.

"I'm sorry," Penelope backpedaled. "I didn't mean to…"

Vivian was moving in toward Brock. Her fingers too rose to the scar. "He led you through battle and you got shot."

"He led us away from harm," he reminded her.

"Not far away enough. He's dead," she reminded him.

It was the first time Penelope had seen some remorse in Vivian's face.

Vivian removed her hand from Brock's skin and looked up at him. "He was a brave man."

"He was."

"You're not the only one he saved."

"No, ma'am. He's credited for saving a lot of people. He was a fine soldier."

"That he was," she said softly before turning toward Penelope. "I'm sorry. I don't mean to be so high strung." Her eyes shifted back to Brock and then back to her. "He's good people," she said before she left the room.

Penelope felt her heart rate begin to slow as the anger slipped away. Brock quickly put back on his shirt.

"She's not sure of me," he said.

"She should be. You're not causing us any harm," Penelope argued.

"She doesn't know that. Her argument is valid."

Penelope looked up at him. "She told you what she thinks about you being here?"

He nodded and took the yellow chair he'd been working on and stacked it with the others he'd assembled.

"I don't blame her. It looks sketchy when you think about it."

She moved toward him as he busied himself with cleaning up. Reaching out her hand, she touched his arm. "For what it's worth, I believe Adam sent you. I don't think his mother had anything to do with it."

He turned his head and smiled. "I appreciate that."

"It was nice of you to come and help assemble. This is starting to look like the daycare we'd planned."

"If I were a kid, I'd want to be here. My sister sent six boxes of books too."

Penelope felt the trembling start in her jaw. "Why?"

"She's a teacher, on sabbatical to raise her kids. They were in her garage and she thought you could put them to use."

"She's not going to teach again?"

"Someday," he said with a shrug. "She'll get more."

The dam broke and tears began to spill. She hated the emotional roller coaster that came with pregnancy. One minute she was going to jump a man because he had a sexy smile and the next she was a blubbering idiot.

"That was very generous," she sobbed.

He moved to her and pulled her into his arms. "Please don't cry."

"I can't help it. It just happens."

His hand brushed over her hair. "Yeah, I remember my sister doing this too."

The front door opened and closed and Penelope turned to see Sam staring at them. "Really, I'll buy more candy if you want."

That made her laugh. "I'm just emotional. Hormones." She wiped her tears. "Look at all of this that Brock did today."

Sam examined the room. "Thank God. I didn't want to have to do all of this."

"His sister sent six boxes of books too."

"Very generous," Sam said looking at Brock.

"I'll finish the chairs today. Tomorrow I can finish the book shelves."

Sam nodded and turned to walk out of the room before turning back. "Will you be here this weekend? I certainly could use some help out back."

Penelope waited for his answer.

"I only have enough to stay in the hotel for a few days. Of course, I'd be happy to help."

"You need a place then?" Sam asked and was answered with a shrug from Brock. "Let me make a few phone calls," he said before he disappeared down the hall.

"I like him," Brock said. "Amelia's a lucky woman."

"We all are." Though who could have thought, that was a true statement? Sam Jackson was the one, initially, to throw them together and that could have been as disastrous.

Penelope stepped back from him. "I'm going to go change."

"Do you have dinner plans?" Brock asked.

Penelope shook her head. "No. We usually just throw something together while we work."

"Can I take you to dinner?"

She clenched her hands and rested them on her stomach to keep them from trembling. "You want to go out?"

"Yeah."

"How about I take you out for helping?" she offered.

"How about we do that some other time? I invited. I'll take you." He gave her a wink with one of those dark eyes. "I'll finish up and wait for you."

Right. That was her cue to go get ready, but she stood there frozen. That was until the urge to kiss him took over, so she did. And when she pulled back, those dark eyes were closed. That was called satisfaction.

Chapter Eleven

Brock assembled another chair and cleaned up the boxes and wrappings he'd accumulated.

"Do you have anything pressing next week?" Sam was standing in the doorway when Brock looked up.

"I don't have any plans yet. I seem to be unemployed and living at my parents' house at this point."

Sam laughed. "The guy who owns the townhouse Vivian is staying in also has a duplex just on the edge of town that is vacant. He said since I got him the settlement against the last tenant, he'd offer it to you for free for a few weeks."

"Really? Someone did that for you?"

"Sure. It's amazing what people will do for you *if* you win for them. And then sometimes when I don't win, I remember why I have a concealed weapons permit."

Brock chuckled. "I appreciate you doing that for me. And I'd be happy to help out. Maybe tomorrow I can get the rest of the shelves up."

"That would be helpful. They'll open for registration soon and we want the place in order. The only part that will still be ugly when they open is the kitchen. But that'll be revamped by the first of the year. There is one more bedroom to fix up and the attic will serve as Amelia's office. At least that's the plan for now."

"What is her role here?"

"I guess administrative. Vivian has the early childhood education and Penelope, well she has the compassion."

Yes, that was it exactly. She had compassion.

"This will be nice for them."

"It will be. I'll miss having Penelope at the office with me, but she needs to be with her baby and Vivian needs to be with the girls. Adam didn't leave them anything. This elevates them having to get jobs and pay for daycare themselves."

Brock still couldn't believe that Sergeant Monroe was the same man they talked about.

"Didn't Sergeant Monroe receive death benefits? He was killed in combat."

Sam nodded. "It helped with all of this. But he had changed his will before he deployed again. He left everything to Amelia."

That wasn't right. How could a man ignore his two children and the one on the way? Then again, how could a man marry more than one woman?

It was obvious that Sergeant Monroe had been a fine soldier, but a lousy husband. Maybe there was more to Sergeant Monroe sending him there. Perhaps he'd sent him on purpose to help take care of Penelope. Why else wouldn't he have just let them send back his items? After all, he knew he was dying.

Brock thought about the times he'd talked with Sergeant Monroe about "back home." He never had much to say, until Penelope came into the picture. From then on it was about the woman he loved. Her beautiful face. Her sweet voice. The baby. Why hadn't he ever mentioned Vivian and the girls? How could a man just discredit them and forget them?

It was becoming clear, he thought. Brock Romero was a man who believed in fate. It was fate that he was the man holding Sergeant Monroe when he died. Though he could have asked for anyone, Sergeant Monroe bestowed his requests on Brock. Now he felt as though his mission in Parson's Gulch, Oklahoma was to continue. He was meant to help the wives of Sergeant Monroe go on—especially Penelope.

"I hope it's okay. I asked Penelope to dinner," he said to Sam, perhaps out of context of their conversation, which was obvious by Sam's change in facial expression.

"Of course. She's allowed to go out to eat." Sam laughed. "You certainly don't need my permission."

"I just didn't want to take her away if you had things you were expecting her to do."

Sam smiled and shook his head. "I'm sure Penelope would rather get out of here while we work. She can't do much but sit and I know that gets to her. It would be nice if you'd take her out for the evening. And tomorrow, stop by my office and get the keys to the duplex. She can tell you how to get there."

"Thank you, sir," Brock said moving toward Sam with his hand extended.

Sam looked at his hand and then back up to him before shaking it. "You can call me Sam. It's okay. And it's nice to have you here. Thank you for all your help."

As Sam walked out of the room, he noticed Penelope descending the stairs. He'd expected her to only change out of her work clothes into something more comfortable, but she'd done much more.

Her hair was pulled back, giving him a perfect view of that slender, beautiful neck. Small pearls dangled from her ears and she wore a sundress, which fell over the rise in her stomach. He was sure she literally glowed. It was no wonder Sergeant Monroe had fallen in love with her. What man wouldn't?

"I think you get more beautiful each time I see you," he said and her cheeks colored pink.

"I feel like a house. I put this on because I'm so hot. I can't get cool enough. And the only shoes that fit are these flip flops because my ankles are swollen." She let out a sigh. "I'm disgusting."

Brock shook his head. "Quite the opposite. You're stunning."

Penelope narrowed her eyes. "What's wrong with you? How can you look at a pregnant woman as if she's not disgusting?"

Brock moved to her and took her hands in his. "There is nothing disgusting about a pregnant woman. Nothing." He bent down to brush a kiss on her lips because he simply couldn't handle not kissing her any longer.

Penelope pulled back. "I'm sorry."

"Don't be," Brock said as he retracted. "I shouldn't have done that."

Penelope looked down and then met his eyes. "Thank you for the flowers. I saw them in the kitchen."

"You're welcome." He let out a breath, desperate to try and kiss her again.

"Let me get washed up and we can go." He moved past her but stopped when she reached out her hand to him.

"The only man who ever gave me attention like this was Adam and you can see where that got me." She rubbed her stomach. "I can't see why you'd want to kiss me."

"Not all men are created equal, Penelope." He turned away and walked to the bathroom to clean up.

As he washed his hands, he looked in the mirror. There was a scar above his eyebrow he'd received when he was nine from a wayward hockey puck. Another scar on his chin from the cement rash after crashing on his bike. One of his eyes was rounder than the other. And he had that single hole still in his ear from when he was eleven and thought he needed to pierce it with a safety pin.

Weren't they all scarred in some way? Penelope was just pregnant. She was carrying a baby. A baby who would never know his father—never have a chance to. He would be loved unconditionally by his mother—but who would love his mother? Who indeed—especially since she didn't think she was worthy?

That needed to change. There was no way Brock could hide how he felt about her. His body went into overdrive every time she was near him. Perhaps that was just part of his mission. To make Penelope Monroe understand that she *was* worthy of a man's appreciation—not just so she'd go to bed with him.

As he dried off his hands, he thought about his own family. His parents had been married for nearly forty years. His brother and sister were both in very solid relationships and bringing new lives into the world. His mother loved to cook—and didn't do it well, but his father still encouraged her. His father loved to garden—but couldn't make anything grow—yet his mother also encouraged him.

Brock had failed one class in school his sophomore year of high school, but instead of grounding him, or taking away his new car, his mother sat with him every night at the table and helped him study until he could pass that class the second time around. Never once did she complain about it either.

Maybe, Penelope needed to meet his family. She needed to see what *his* normal was like. Perhaps she'd trust him just a little more. That was if he could keep his hands off her.

He laughed when he thought about it. How could she possibly think that being pregnant made her disgusting? Nothing was further from the truth.

~*~

Penelope figured she'd eaten too many candy bars at work. Her stomach was unsettled and she just wasn't hungry. Brock, on the other hand, was scraping the spaghetti off his plate with a piece of bread.

She watched him enjoy his dinner. She'd never been much of a cook. Oh, she could throw a few decent things together. The fact that she'd never starved spoke volumes. Her mother wasn't much of a cook either. When would she have time to cook? Frozen dinners shoved in the microwave or drive-thru meals were the dinners Penelope could remember.

She decided right then and there she was going to learn to cook. From what Brock had told her it looked like he'd be sticking around for a few weeks to help them get the daycare together. Sam had secured him a place to live.

He deserved a good meal once in awhile for helping. She'd see that he got one.

"Is your mother a good cook? My mother never had time to cook."

He looked up at her with his mouth full of spaghetti and smiled with noodles hanging out of his mouth. Brock slurped them up, wiped his mouth, and took a sip from his beer.

"Are you asking me that because I'm devouring this?"

She shook her head. "No. I just wondered."

He smiled and the dimple in his cheek deepened— which had to be the most fantastic part of his smile.

"Don't ever tell her I told you this, but no. My mother can't cook to save her soul, but she tries. She loves to cook. She loves to feed people, but it never turns out well."

"And you've never told her this?"

"And break her heart? No way." He smiled again and this time there was a sparkle in his eyes, which could only have been there because he loved his mother that much.

"If it's bad, do you eat it?"

"Every bite. She gets such pleasure out of us eating her food. We just take very little portions."

"You do all of that just to make your mother happy?"

His eyes narrowed. "Of course. Wouldn't you?"

No. No, she wouldn't. Her mother wouldn't have noticed if she'd eaten or not. As they sat at the table for dinner, her mother would have had her laptop right next to her checking on the progress of this project or another. Penelope would either watch TV, which her mother would allow as long as the volume was low or she'd have had her nose in a book.

They'd coexisted, but they hadn't shared their life together. In fact, her mother must have been so busy that she hadn't even checked in on her daughter or her grandbaby. Penelope could only assume they were out of her hair and that was okay.

"Are you going to eat your meatball?" Brock asked with his mouth still full.

Penelope shook her head. "Please, go ahead." She pushed her plate toward him and he stabbed the ball and set it on his plate.

"Aren't you hungry?"

"No. I'm sorry. I have a lot on my mind I guess."

Brock gave her a small shrug. "They'll box it up for you. There's nothing better than cold spaghetti in the middle of the night."

Once Brock had finished the basket of bread, his meal, four bites of hers, and drank down his beer, he sat back in his chair and rested his hands on his stomach.

"I'm going to have to go for a run in the morning. I'm going to gain thirty pounds if I'm not careful. But I've really missed good food."

"Amelia runs at six o'clock every morning. Then she'd head to the rec center to work out, but now she can do that in the basement."

"She has a gym in the basement?"

Penelope smiled and nodded. "We built it for her. She made sure that Vivian and I were taken care of and our children were too. Adam left everything to her. She could have walked away with everything, but she didn't. She uprooted her life and stayed here—with us."

"And her and Sam?"

"Oh, they fell in love fast. It was a little risky on his part," she considered. "He could have gotten in a lot of trouble, being Adam's lawyer and all."

"He's a decent guy."

"Oh, he's more than decent. He's—well—he's extraordinary." She rested her hands on her stomach as the baby moved. "They're going to be very happy together."

Brock leaned in over the table. "What about you? Does it bother you?"

"Should it?" She tried to keep her voice steady. Yes, it bothered her that she wouldn't have what Amelia had. But Vivian didn't have it either. She had just figured it was a trade for not having children.

"No. It shouldn't. You're a beautiful woman and you won't be alone for long."

That caused her to snort out a laugh. "I'm six months pregnant. It'll be a while before I start turning the heads of men."

Brock pursed his lips and leaned in even further. He reached out his hand as if in invitation to hold hers. After a moment, she slid her hand into his.

"Not all men are put off by a pregnant woman. I think it's becoming on you."

She sucked in a breath and tried to keep calm. "Yes, but this doesn't go away. When I'm not pregnant then, I'll be a mother. I'll have a baby attached to me always. I'll be nursing and sleep deprived."

"And just as beautiful and wonderful as you are now."

She didn't want to hear this. She couldn't hear it. Brock Romero was passing through. He might be staying for a while, but it wouldn't last.

He was fulfilling a promise and he was doing a fine job. But he was just homesick for the normal. In time, she figured, he'd tire of her body—her needs—and he'd decide to move on.

The waitress set the check and a carryout box on the table. Brock pulled his hand back to reach into his pocket for his wallet. He set a number of dollars with the bill and then tucked his wallet back into his pocket.

"C'mon, let's pack up that dinner and head back. You look tired."

Because she didn't want to discuss how beautiful he thought she was and how ugly she felt, she simply nodded and began to pack up her dinner.

But wouldn't it be wonderful, she thought as she slid the noodles from the plate to the box. For a moment, she could imagine Brock Romero being sincere and wanting her. And wouldn't it be a dream come true to be part of a family like his?

She squeezed her eyes shut. She was setting herself up for disappointment. It would be better to not think about it at all. She'd done that once. She'd bought into Adam's words and promises. There was no reason to assume Brock Romero was any different.

Chapter Twelve

Why did hotel rooms always have to be either so damn hot or so damn cold? There was no comfortable middle ground, Brock thought as he kicked back the sheets again, in an attempt to cool himself.

Admittedly, he knew it might not be the room at all. It was probably just his mind still going a million miles a minute. It used to do that when he'd lie there in his tent with his gun strapped to his chest.

When he'd returned home from dinner with Penelope, he'd called his mother. He stifled a laugh when she'd told him she'd made the best meatloaf ever. Okay, her meatloaf was probably one of her better dishes, but still, he could only imagine his father's heartburn.

He'd told her he planned on staying longer in Oklahoma than he'd planned and she'd grown quiet.

"Brock, are you seeing someone?"

A smile had formed on his lips. "I'm just helping out Sergeant Monroe's family, Ma. But I won't lie. There is a girl here, but she's not very interested in me right now. But I was thinking," he bit down on the side of his cheek. "I think she could do with a dose of family—real family—for a weekend. Would you be okay if I brought her home with me for a visit?"

"Oh, Brock, you know you're welcome to do that anytime. But, doesn't she have any family?"

"Not like ours," he said and thought not many people did. "She has some very close friends here," or so they appeared to be close. Hadn't he assumed both Vivian and Amelia would have taken him down had he done her wrong? "She needs a little of your fussing, dad's jokes and some sibling banter."

"I'll make up the spare room and you just tell me when you're coming."

He could hear the sincerity in her voice and he'd expected nothing less. "Thanks, Ma. I'll come up in a few weeks and I'll send you pictures of this old house they're fixing up. You would love it. It reminds me of Great-Grandma's house."

"That was a shame to have to sell. I'm glad they're not having to sell that one." He heard what he assumed was a stifled sob. "I miss you, Brocky. I only got a few hours with you. And I'm not trying to make you feel bad, I just want you to know."

"I know, Ma. I miss you too. Give Dad a hug for me."

When the sun peeked through the dingy curtains, he knew it was too early to head to the house. If he was lucky, he'd slept until six o'clock. Thinking of all the food he'd eaten in the past few days he considered that he'd better put on some running shoes and hit the pavement—and so he did.

A mile into his run he realized he was running toward the house on Main and Pine. Another mile in, he was running up Main and he could see Amelia running down Main.

He gave her a wave as she stopped in front of the house.

"You're up early," she said, stretching from side to side.

He worked to catch a breath so he could talk. "Couldn't sleep."

She scanned a look over him and narrowed her eyes on him. "You up for some sparring?"

As interesting as that sounded, he wasn't sure he was. It was too early to think about sparring—especially a woman.

Amelia had fisted her hands on her hips and waited for him to answer. "If you're scared…"

"I'm not scared. I just don't want to hurt you. I'm not one to spar with women."

A crooked grin formed on her lips and her eyes sparkled. "Don't worry about me. If I thought I'd get in trouble with it I wouldn't have offered. But you can take it easy on me if you want to. It's just one hell of a workout."

That it was. "Okay, let's go."

She gave him a full on grin now and started toward the house. He couldn't help but wonder if Penelope was up and in the kitchen. After all, he couldn't have accidently run that way if she hadn't crept into his subconscious, right?

Amelia led him into the house and back to the kitchen. The house was quiet and to his dismay, Penelope wasn't there waiting for him.

The thought made him laugh to himself as he followed Amelia down the stairs to the basement. When she flicked on the lights, he actually gasped.

"You do have a whole gym down here."

She nodded. "Can you believe they did this for me?"

"Well, from what I understand you've done a lot for them."

She shrugged and fixed her ponytail by separating it and giving it a yank. "What he did wasn't right. I'd never be able to live with myself if those kids suffered. I know what it's like to lose a parent in combat. They don't deserve that."

Amelia threw him a pair of sparring gloves and a helmet.

Brock secured the gloves and wondered if his head would fit in the helmet. "Your father died in combat?"

"Oh, such small minded people always assume that." She put on her helmet, and then secured her gloves. "My mother died in Desert Storm. My father raised us."

He'd known enough strong women whom he'd served with, and he knew he'd been wrong to assume such a thing. "I'm sorry. I'll bet she was a fine soldier."

"Of course she was." Amelia gave him a nod. "Ready?"

"Sure, but really I don't want to hurt..." The words hadn't even come out of his mouth when he realized he was flat on his back looking up at the basement ceiling.

She was standing over him looking down at him. "Are you okay? Did I hurt you?"

Brock let out a groan and she laughed.

"I take that as you're okay?" she asked and he nodded. "Another round?"

Brock rolled to his side and then to his knees. "Another round?" he asked as he got to his feet. "I don't think that counted."

"One point for me. Stay on your feet."

"Easy for you to say."

She was grinning. "I don't do well with men who won't fight me," she said as she danced around him. "I invited you to the match, I'll fight you evenly."

He still wasn't sure about this, but then he ducked her punch.

"Good. You do know how to do this," she said as he blocked a roundhouse kick aimed for his ribs.

"Oh, I know how to do it. I've just never done it with a woman."

"I won't tell Penelope," she laughed as she struck out with a back-fist aimed at his head followed by a left punch, which landed right in his chest.

Brock staggered back and pressed his gloved hand to where she'd hit him.

"Amelia, what are you doing?" Penelope's voice shrieked through the basement.

Brock looked up to see her standing there in a nightshirt that clung to the very feminine curves of her body.

"Don't panic. I invited him to spar and he's too afraid to hit me. So I'm kicking his ass."

"I was taught not to hit girls," he said in retort to her statement.

"You know, girls start fights too. Look at how many men have had to chase down their dismembered parts because of a woman."

"Amelia!" Penelope screeched again.

"I'm not sure how she got pregnant. She's really a prude."

He watched as Penelope's face began to grow redder. He pulled the helmet from his head. "I could do with some coffee. Do you mind if I make some?"

Amelia shook her head. "You're done already?"

"I think so."

She nodded. "I'd love some coffee. Yell down when it's done."

Brock pulled the gloves from his hands, tucked them into the helmet, and set them in the corner. He followed Penelope up to the kitchen and could hear Amelia begin her assault on the heavy bag.

"Did she hurt you?" Penelope asked the moment he cleared the last step.

"No."

"She used to train soldier's wives to defend themselves against their husbands. The first time she met Adam she kicked his butt too."

He laughed and moved toward the coffee pot. "She's very strong." He pulled out the pot and began to fill it with water at the sink. "I heard that her mother died in combat."

"Yes. Those are some big shoes to fill."

"You're right." He turned off the water and began to fill the coffee maker. "Speaking of mothers—I asked mine if she'd mind if you came for a visit with me."

"You what?" Her voice was sharp. "Why do you want me to go visit your mother? I don't really know you."

Brock could feel anger rise in him at her reaction, but he focused on the task at hand to calm himself. Filter. Coffee—two scoops. Close the filter lid. Press brew. Breathe in. Breathe out.

By the time he turned to look at her he was calmer, but by the look on her face she wasn't.

"You don't have to make the trip with me. It was only a thought—a kind invitation," he said as calmly as he could.

Her lip trembled and she adjusted the nightshirt as if she finally realized what she was wearing. "I just met you."

"I understand that."

"I still don't understand why you want to be around me. I'm someone else's discarded, pregnant wife. I have nothing to offer a man."

She was batting her eyes and he could see the moisture on her lashes. Why did he have to always make her cry?

Brock took a step toward her then stopped. "You weren't discarded."

"Sure I was. He didn't choose me the first time he met me and marrying was a game to him. It doesn't make a woman feel very worthwhile."

He took the few steps to get closer to her. "What do you mean he didn't choose you the first time?"

Her lips twitched and her eyes batted faster. "We met him at a bar one night, an ex-friend and I. She went home with him."

Brock felt the last bit of respect he held for the man plummet to the bottom of his stomach. "He was taking girls home from the bar?"

Penelope nodded. "That should have been that. I should have forgotten all about it, but I couldn't. The next time I saw him he was talking to *me*. He knew I was a virgin and was waiting for marriage and he just wooed me."

He hadn't heard that word in a long time—wooed? But what he heard loud and clear was that Sergeant Monroe was a player and Penelope had been played.

Despite the kisses they'd shared—and especially the ones she'd planted on him—he knew he had to tread carefully on the subject. He wasn't just dealing with a woman scorned by a man. He was dealing with a pregnant widow of a lying, cheating man.

She was wiping at those moist eyes now and he couldn't let her cry without offering some kind of support.

Brock pulled her to him and held her against his chest. Her blonde curls went in all directions so he smoothed over them with his hand.

"Think about going home with me. Nothing more than a few days away from here. I want you to meet my family and to just be around family. My sister has kids and my sister-in-law is pregnant too. You'd have someone to talk to about it."

She eased against him and he closed his eyes. Months of looking at her face in pictures hadn't prepared him for actually holding her in his arms.

"I will warn you," he said on a laugh. "My mother will try to feed you. You'll want to take small portions."

She giggled against his chest and looked up at him. "My mother never cooked for me. I'm guessing your mother's bad cooking beats that."

In that moment he knew this wasn't just looking at her face in pictures or fulfilling a promise, there was more. *He* wanted to take care of her and give her a life with no missing pieces.

Chapter Thirteen

When the tears had dried Penelope had become very aware that she was still in her pajamas, teeth unbrushed, and her hair a mass of unruly curls. As quickly as she'd run down the stairs when she heard the commotion in the basement, she retreated to get ready.

Brock found a mug and poured a cup of coffee. And because he could hear Amelia on the steps, he poured one for her too and had it in his hand when she finally showed herself.

"I'm not very sneaky, huh?" She smiled as she reached for the mug.

"You might be just fine. I'm trained to hear everything."

Amelia nodded and sipped. "You want to take her home and meet your family? That sounds like a relationship thing. You just met her."

Brock decided that his week as a civilian had dampened his senses. He hadn't heard Amelia until Penelope had left the room. But she must have been on the stairs for a long time.

"I think a dose of real family would do her some good. I want her to see not every man was raised by a mother like Sergeant Monroe's. Or a neglectful one, like her own."

"She doesn't talk about her mother much."

"I don't think there's much to say," he said as he sipped at his own coffee.

He was fully aware that they would protect Penelope against anyone. Whatever the bond was between them was strong and he was a stranger.

Brock set his coffee on the counter and crossed his arms over his chest.

"I know that Mrs. Monroe—Vivian—doesn't trust my reasons for being here. I want you to know though, I don't mean anyone any harm."

Amelia nodded slowly. "She's vulnerable right now."

"I know that. And I'll admit I might have shown up here already half in love with her. That doesn't help."

Now he'd turned Amelia against him. He saw it in the stance she took when she turned and set her mug on the kitchen table.

His first response was to stand away from the counter and prepare his body for a battle. It took more willpower to remain at ease, leaned against the counter—arms crossed.

"What the hell does that mean?" She was moving toward him now, but he remained at ease.

"I carried her pictures for months. I built her up in my mind. What else was I supposed to do? She got me through my recovery. Knowing I'd be coming here to meet her and give her what Sergeant Monroe asked me to, kept my spirits up."

"You said in love."

"I did. I don't mean I think she loves me or that I am, in fact, in love with her. I just have the advantage here."

"Now you sound like him."

And that made him stand up straight. "In no way did I mean to. I came here thinking he was an upstanding man, but I've changed my mind."

Her jaw twitched and she took a step back. "A good solider. Not an upstanding man."

Brock nodded. "I'll agree with you there."

Amelia paced the kitchen. "You're good for her. Vivian doesn't think so, but I do."

That hurt, though he wasn't sure why it was important for them all to like him, but he'd like to have Vivian's approval too. "I want to be good for her. I want to be here for her and the baby."

Now Amelia's eyes narrowed on him. "What does that give you?"

His shoulders dropped. "Give me?"

"What man meets a woman and suddenly wants to take on her unborn child?"

Was that what he'd said? "I meant that I want to be a good male role model for her baby. Penelope didn't have a man in her life, but I think her baby should."

"And you're volunteering to take that position?"

"I think I'd be a fine prospect."

"Like a job?"

"Like something I think is important and I'd like to do."

The scowl slipped away and there was something in her eyes that said he'd answered correctly. "How long have your parents been married?"

"Nearly forty years."

"You have siblings?"

"A brother and a sister." He knew where she was going now and he was just going to beat her to the punch. "My sister and her husband have three children and my brother and his wife are expecting their first."

That something in her eyes was a sparkle and it was bright now and so was the smile that formed on her lips. "You come from a good family."

"The best if you ask me."

Amelia turned and picked up her coffee. "I'm sorry. I'm sure you can understand why we are a little hesitant."

"I would be too. But I will never—ever—hurt her."

"That's a lot to ask from anyone."

"That's a promise I can keep."

As he turned to pick up his mug, they both heard Penelope scream from the top of the stairs.

They both set their mugs down as they ran for her just as the front door opened and Vivian walked through.

"What's going on?" She was right behind them as they started up.

"I saw a mouse! I saw a mouse!" Penelope screamed and all three of them stopped on the top step and just looked at her.

"Are you kidding me?" Amelia's eyes went wide and her breath hard. "You screamed because of that?"

Penelope's lips tightened. "It scared me."

Brock wanted to laugh, but that wasn't nice so he stifled it as he cleared the first step. "Where did it go?"

Penelope pointed to the room across the hallway.

Brock nodded and walked to the room opening the door. There were boxes stored against the walls and a few pieces of old furniture.

Amelia followed behind him. "This is the next item to fix. It'll be the office."

He looked around. "Well, it looks like we should get it started soon." He pointed to the corner. "There is the hole."

He walked toward the wall where the trim had been gnawed away. Brock knocked on the wall and above them he heard the scattering.

"Oh, God! They're in the attic!" Penelope had nearly jumped on Vivian.

"I'll go look," he offered and walked out into the hallway.

Just as he pulled the rope to the stairs, all three women yelled, "Wait!" But it was too late. The wall of steps came crashing toward him giving him only a moment to step out of their way.

The air was thick and they all looked at him.

"I'll fix those today," he said.

Amelia nodded. "You're lucky it didn't hit you. Sam wasn't so fortunate."

"Sam got hit by that?" They all nodded. "That could kill someone."

Brock stepped onto the first step and felt the stairs shift under his weight.

"Is there a light up here or do you have a flashlight?"

"There is a switch just to the right at the top," Vivian said as she watched him.

He gave them a nod and started up the steps. When he reached the top, he felt for the switch, hoping nothing would bite him first.

As soon as he hit the light the room above him illuminated with white Christmas lights strung from side to side.

"Have any of you been up here?" He looked down at three shaking heads.

"No," Amelia said. "As soon as Sam tried and the stairs hit him we didn't go back up."

"Well, it's really pretty." He continued up until he was in the small, dusty room. "Someone used this space once as a library or something."

He looked around at the shelves of books and the small couch by the window that looked out over the front of the house. It was certainly filled with storage items, which someone had recently stacked near the opening, but once it was a room someone enjoyed.

Brock looked down as Vivian started up the steps, followed by Penelope and then Amelia.

Vivian looked around taking in the sight.

Penelope coughed and his instinct was to move quickly to her. She smiled at him and moved closer.

Amelia stopped as she cleared the step. "This is awesome. Who would have done this?"

"Adam's grandmother," Vivian said looking around. "She was a German Jew, who had survived the Holocaust as a child. During the years of hiding, she read a lot. That became a source of security to her. The older she became and her mind began to slip, she would hide with books. This is where she hid."

"This is incredible," Penelope said moving toward the bookshelves filled with classic titles. "Some of these are original."

"I think she was afraid Adam's mother would sell them if she knew where they were."

Penelope's eyes narrowed. "But the house belonged to his father's mother."

Vivian nodded. "You've encountered her. It's exactly like her. It didn't matter who it belonged to."

Brock moved toward the wall where he was sure the mice would climb from the other room. He moved the newly placed boxes out of the way and Amelia pushed them closer toward the light in the center of the room.

"These aren't very dusty," she said as she pulled open the top to the first box. Brock watched as she pulled out envelope after envelope. "These are all sealed."

Amelia looked at the front of the letters and her shoulders dropped as she looked at Vivian.

"What's wrong?" Vivian moved toward her, ripping the envelopes out of her hand. "What in the hell?"

She dropped down to her knees and pulled out another handful of envelopes. "Son-of-a-bitch!"

Penelope moved toward them. "What is it?"

Vivian looked up. Tears had filled her eyes as she clutched the letters to her chest. "They're letters to me from Adam."

Chapter Fourteen

There were three boxes of letters that Brock helped Amelia and Vivian carry down to the kitchen. In each box, there were years of letters never given to Vivian.

"What are you going to do with these?" Penelope asked as she followed them all down the stairs.

"I'm going to read them. And then I'm going to pay his mother a visit," she said through gritted teeth.

"I want to be there," Amelia said taking out a letter that had been postmarked six years earlier. "I'll bet you could scare the woman to death just by showing up on her doorstep with one of these letters."

"And the watch she accused me of stealing," Vivian added.

Penelope moved in and picked up a letter. "Why would she hide these here? If you were going to steal letters why not just throw them away?" They all looked at her and she shrugged. "I mean this way you risk getting caught."

Brock sat down at the table and studied the women looking at the letters. "Do you think she wanted to get caught?"

Three sets of eyes looked his way.

"Are you kidding me?" Vivian snapped. "She'd want to get caught?"

He raised his hands in surrender. "Hear me out. People like her need attention. I knew that from the minute she went hysterical when I called looking for Penelope." He gave her a small smile when he saw her gazing in his direction. "This gave her control over you—and him. Maybe you'll find out just how much control if you read them in order."

He could literally see Vivian deflate as she let out a breath. "You think everything that has happened was because of her?"

Brock shrugged. "Maybe in some little way. I'm just saying that when you read these maybe you'll see him differently."

All three sets of eyes were still on him, but he couldn't help it. No matter what horrible things Sergeant Monroe seemed to have done, he'd saved Brock's life and he'd never forget that. And maybe, just maybe, there had been a shred of decency in the man. Maybe.

Penelope had gone into the office when Vivian began to sort through letters and Brock started to assemble furniture. Amelia had followed her and was in Sam's office with the last of the papers they needed to go over before they began taking on registrations for the daycare.

The plan was to open to registration the following week.

It gave Penelope a nervous, yet giddy tingle to think that the three, well four, of them, had updated the old house and in a month is would be full of little ones. It was a big honor to think that parents would entrust their loved ones with them. It was a huge responsibility too.

Of course, she was no stranger to facing responsibility, she thought as the baby shifted, and it caused her to do the same. She rubbed her stomach and thought—this little one would be all her responsibility. What kind of mother would she be?

Already, thanks to Amelia, she could ensure that she'd be an attentive mother. She wouldn't have to work away from her baby. There was the promise of a roof over her head and good companionship when she needed it. The baby already had siblings—something Penelope didn't have. And then there was Brock.

Penelope let out a slow breath and rubbed the ache in her side away. She'd been hard on him that morning when he asked her to go visit his parents. But now when she thought about it, he'd had her best interest in mind. Oh, she'd probably looked like an idiot. She'd kiss him then blow him off. And then she'd do it all over again. How did any man love a woman through her pregnancy?

And that thought stopped her.

He didn't love her. He was a compassionate man and she was stupid. But she really liked him and by all accounts it seemed as though he liked her too.

Maybe before the daycare opened she should go back to visit his parents with him. She could see what a real family was like and she could see what he was like. Who was Brock Romero when he wasn't fulfilling a last wish? In his parents' home he'd wouldn't be able to BS her if he, in fact, ever had.

It would also give Amelia and Vivian time away from her. She knew she was a lot of work and both of them worried about her constantly. However, that did give her a lot of comfort. No one else had ever fussed over her before. If nothing else, she owed Adam for that.

The door to the office opened and she sat up in her chair. Did it say something about the man when Brock walked into the office and her heart picked up its pace?

"Hey," he said smiling as he shut the door. "Sam told me to come by and get the key to the duplex where I can stay."

Penelope nodded because for the life of her she couldn't even think of something to say in his presence. She'd been stupid this morning to jump all over his invitation and she knew she looked like a fool. But he was standing there smiling at her and looking at her with great contentment. Hadn't he noticed that she'd been flip-flopping over her reaction to him?

"Everything okay?" he asked inching toward her desk.

Penelope nodded. "Let me go get Sam. He's in his office with Amelia."

"Oh, I can wait if he needs me to."

And she was sure he would. He was that kind of man. "His door is open. That means he doesn't mind if I interrupt."

She maneuvered, less than gracefully, out of her chair and walked down the hall to Sam's office. Penelope tapped on the door and both Amelia and Sam looked up at her.

"Brock is here for the key," she said softly and Sam gave her a nod as he walked from the table where he and Amelia worked, to his desk.

"I'll come talk to him," he said as he moved toward her. But just as he made it to the door and Penelope turned to walk back to the lobby, a pain ripped through her side and had her reaching for him, her breath caught in her chest.

"Whoa!" Sam grabbed hold of her and she was very aware of Brock coming toward her and Amelia right behind her.

She let out short breaths just like the ones she'd been reading about when another pain shot through her.

Brock was no longer just in front of her, he was next to her, scooping her up into his arms and somewhere between them they had discussed taking her to the hospital, but she'd never heard anything but her own breathing.

As Brock carried her out of the building, another pain pierced her stomach and this time she let out a yelp as Sam opened the door to Brock's truck and he slid her inside.

"We're right behind you," Amelia said as she put her phone to her ear and she and Sam disappeared.

"Where are we going?" She asked as Brock climbed in next to her and she panted against the pain.

"To the hospital. I think you're in labor."

"I'm not ready to be in labor. I'm too early. Way too early…" But another wave of pain had her reaching for her stomach and holding on for dear life as Brock sped away from the office building.

Brock had hidden behind bushes, crumbling walls, and under tanks during gunfire, yet he'd never been as scared as he was at that very moment.

Penelope's breaths were quick pants and he knew she was as nervous as he was. The baby wasn't due for almost three months.

"I just realized I have no idea where I'm going," he said as he got to the stop sign.

Sam pulled up behind him and Amelia rolled down her window. "What are you doing? Go!"

"I don't know where I'm going," he yelled back.

Sam gave him a nod and pulled out in front of him. Brock followed and within six minutes and twenty-four seconds they were at the door to the emergency clinic.

Brock slammed the truck into park and ran to the other side where Amelia had already pulled open the door.

"Are you okay?" She asked and Penelope only nodded. "I'm going to get you a wheelchair and Sam is already inside telling them you're here."

Amelia turned and hurried for the door as Brock scooped her up and followed.

"Brock, I think it's over. I think I'm okay." Her voice was weak and he didn't like it.

"We're taking you in and making sure."

She rested her head against his shoulder and he placed a kiss on her head. He wasn't going to let anything happen to them. In his heart, he knew this was where he was supposed to be. Sergeant Monroe might have asked him to simply find her and deliver the box, but there was so much more. He wasn't so manly that he couldn't admit—at least to himself—he was in love with her and the baby. It would devastate him to lose either one of them.

Amelia moved toward him as he walked through the door. She pushed the wheelchair to him and he gently set Penelope down.

Her skin was pale and her eyes sunken. Something was wrong. He looked up to see Vivian walking through the door with a girl holding each hand.

"Is she okay? What happened? Why is she still right here? She should be with a doctor." She walked right past them and to the counter where Sam was still talking to the woman behind the desk. "She needs a doctor right now. I'm not going to have her sitting here waiting. The baby needs attention and so does she. Where is Doctor Barker? I saw his car and he needs to see her right now."

Brock watched as Sam tilted his head to look at her and a smile crossed his lips before he looked back at the woman behind the desk.

"I'm calling him right now. I swear he'll be right out. I'll take you back to a room for observation."

"That's better," Vivian said as she turned back around.

"I think we should get you a law degree. I could use you in my office," Sam joked as the woman walked toward Penelope.

"Who is the father?" The woman looked at the group that had formed around Penelope.

Amelia stepped forward, her eyes narrow. "We all go back."

The woman shook her head. "No. Only one."

All eyes shifted to Brock when Penelope reached up and took his hand. He swallowed hard and gritted his teeth to keep them from chattering.

"Okay then," the nurse acknowledged Penelope's movement as she began to push her down the hallway and Brock, his hand still grasped in Penelope's, jogged to keep up.

The nurse pushed Penelope into a room. The pain had subsided, but she kept reminding herself to breathe—though she was beginning to feel light headed.

"Can you help her onto the bed?" The nurse looked at Brock as she pulled a monitor from the corner.

Brock stood in front of her. "Can you stand?"

Penelope held her hands up for him to take and he helped her out of the chair. Gingerly, he moved her to the bed and eased her down.

His eyes were wide and she knew the look of fear. Did he really worry that something was wrong?

Penelope lay back against the raised bed, her hands on both sides of her stomach. "Thank you."

"For what?"

"Being here. I need you here."

"I'll never be anywhere else." He cupped her face. "You'll let me stay?"

"Please," she croaked out. She needed him. She wanted him. There wasn't a moment she wanted to turn him away again.

The nurse moved in next to the bed and Brock shifted to the other side. She lifted Penelope's shirt and attached a monitor to her stomach.

As she started up the machine, she asked Penelope the routine questions about what had happened and why she was there. A moment later the doctor walked through the door.

"Having a little excitement today are we?" He smiled at Penelope as he walked over to her. "Let's look at the baby and make sure everything is okay."

He moved the ultrasound machine from the corner and Penelope reached for Brock's hand and squeezed.

"It's all okay," he whispered to her as he ran his other hand over her hair. "I'm here."

He would be too, she thought. Brock Romero seemed to be exactly that man who did what he said he'd do.

As the doctor spread the gel on her stomach, she realized she was holding her breath. The room was silent as the doctor moved the wand over her stomach.

"No bleeding?"

Penelope's lips trembled. "No."

She felt a wave ripple through her stomach again, though much different than before.

"Whoa," the doctor grinned as it happened. "Alrighty. Looks like this little one is anxious to meet you."

"No!" Penelope felt her heart rate quicken. "It's too soon."

The doctor patted her arm. "You're right. We're going to make sure you're comfortable and so is the baby. These are called Braxton Hicks contractions. False labor. Here," he said as he turned up the volume on the monitor. "The baby sounds healthy and looks good."

Penelope fixed her stare on the monitor. She'd been nearly too preoccupied with the thought that something had gone wrong that she hadn't noticed that the doctor had a perfect picture of the baby's face on the screen.

She felt the warmth of the tears on her cheeks before she even realized she was crying.

Brock leaned down next to her. "That has to be the most beautiful thing I've ever seen," he whispered in her ear.

She wanted to comment, but she couldn't. The tears kept rolling and Brock stayed right next to her as the doctor took a few more measurements and then printed out the picture.

"Here's another one for the baby's album." He handed her the picture and wiped the gel from her stomach. "I'm going to order an IV and get you hydrated. I want you to relax and get comfortable for a few hours. I'll be back in to check on you after the IV."

Brock stood and held his hand out to the doctor. "Thank you, sir. Thank you for taking care of her."

The doctor smiled as he shook his hand. "She's doing great and it looks like she's got a good support team," he chuckled as he nodded toward the door where Vivian and Amelia's faces were pressed to the window.

Brock rested his hand on Penelope's shoulder. "She sure does."

Penelope had never been a big fan of needles and when she saw the one coming toward her to insert the IV she thought she was going to be ill.

Brock leaned in close and turned her head toward him. He pressed a gentle kiss to her cheek. "I've never asked you. Do you have names picked out for the baby?"

"Not really. I don't have any family names. I always like the name Shelby, you know like the girl in *Steel Magnolias.*"

He nodded. "Right. And if I remember they were going to use that name for the baby if it were a girl or a boy."

Penelope nodded slightly with her head now pressed to Brock's.

"What are your parent's names?" she asked.

"My mom's name is Gwen. Short for Gwendolyn."

"Oh, I really like that."

He brushed his hand over her head. "And my dad's name is Gregory."

Penelope let out a low hum. "I really like that too."

"Okay, all done," the nurse said as she adjusted the tubes that led to the IV.

Penelope looked at her arm. "It didn't hurt that bad."

The nurse gave her a smile and a wink. "You have a good man there. He kept you occupied." She patted Penelope's leg. "Rest. If you need anything just push the button. But this should help you."

As she walked out of the room, Penelope turned toward Brock. "I thought that would hurt more."

"It usually does."

"I don't know why you're so good to me."

Brock sat on the edge of the bed and pressed his lips to her fingers, which were still folded with his.

"Remember all those pictures that I brought back to you? The ones you'd sent to Sergeant Monroe?" She nodded. "I had them with me for months." He let out a long, deep sigh. "I still have one."

She stared up at him. "You do?"

Brock nodded. "I'm not very proud of it, but I stole one—I guess you could say." He bit down on his lip. "Sergeant Monroe died in my arms and that wore heavy in my heart. I was the last person to talk to this man. This man who saved my life."

Brock wiped his forehead with the back of his other hand. "My blood was still on his hands when he died in my arms."

"Brock…"

"He entrusted me with his final wish, his final words—with you."

The tears were back and she let them fall.

Brock wiped them away. "I kept those pictures on me from the moment he gave them to me until I gave them to you. Your smile and your gaze got me through everything. After they did surgery on my arm, it was your face I saw first."

"I don't know what to say."

"Nothing. I owe you. You got me through the past few months and you don't even know it."

She felt the cold from the IV course through her and a warmth that was brought on by anger at what he'd said.

"You owe me?"

"Yes. Without the thought of you, I don't know if I'd be—well—okay."

She clenched her jaw. "So you're here because you owe me?"

Brock's eyes narrowed on her. "I'm here because I want to be. Why are you upset?"

"I'm upset because I want you to be here with me because of something else. You're still here because you promised Adam you would be."

"That's not true."

"Sure it is. You're here because Adam asked you to be. You're a good enough man to follow through on your word."

"Okay, so I'm here because he asked me to come."

Her teeth began to chatter and her muscles shook from the liquid pumping into her. "And you came back because you promised to help with the daycare."

"Yes."

"Then why are you right here? Why are you going through this with me?"

"Penelope," he cupped her face in his hands. "What do you want me to say?"

She shook her head and turned from him. "Never mind."

Brock stood from the edge of the bed. "I'm going to let the others in. I'm just upsetting you and you don't need to be upset."

She'd have argued with him again if he hadn't been so quick to open the door. The others were just on the other side and they were quickly asking Brock questions.

She took the moment to dry her eyes and try to regain some composure. The fact that she knew what she wanted him to say—and she knew how irrational it was to want him to say it—simply made her queasy.

How much longer could she blame hormones for making her act and feel like such an idiot? A man like Brock Romero would be by her side forever if he promised someone he would be. But she wanted more. And to be lying in a hospital bed connected to an IV because she was six months pregnant wasn't very becoming. Add petty and stupid to the mix and she was becoming unattractive to even herself.

Vivian moved to her quickly. "Are you okay?"

Penelope nodded. "False labor."

"I had that. You're going to be okay."

Amelia patted Penelope's leg. "I guess Adam's kids just can't wait to get here."

When Vivian laughed, Penelope couldn't help but laugh too. Then she looked around. Sam and the girls hadn't come in, but Brock hadn't come back in either.

Amelia sat down at the edge of the bed. "Everything else okay? You look upset and so did Brock."

Penelope turned her head. "I'm just out of sorts. I keep forgetting I'm pregnant with another man's baby and he's fulfilling a promise. My body seems to want more and it isn't fair to assume someone would want that."

Vivian pulled the chair from against the wall over next to the bed. "Brock doesn't want to be part of this?"

Penelope shrugged. "I don't know what he wants. I don't know what I want."

"I think you need to just feel things out. He's here isn't he?"

Penelope gathered the sheet in her hands and twisted. "But why is he here? Because Adam asked him to be."

Amelia let out a grunt. "Well, maybe that in itself was the most decent thing Adam ever did. He sent you a nice man."

She looked at Vivian waiting for her to snap at Amelia's comment, but she hadn't. Was that what Adam had done really?

"He told me he owed me. He said that I was the reason he made it through everything. He carried my pictures with him and without me..."

"He told us."

Penelope tried to sit up, but her body didn't like that. "He told you that?"

They both nodded. "He's afraid he's worked it up in his head that he loves you and you wouldn't feel the same way."

The liquid in her veins grew colder.

Vivian pulled the blanket over her. "You need to not worry about this right now. You need to rest."

She nodded and closed her eyes, but how could she possibly not worry about it? The man had been in her life for a week, but she'd been in his life for months. There was some unfair advantage there. And yet everything inside of her said to take a chance with him.

Gritting her teeth against the chatter that wanted to take over, she willed herself to calm. When he walked back through the door, they'd talk. Yes, that's what they'd do.

Chapter Fifteen

Vivian slapped Amelia on the shoulder to wake her as Penelope purposely looked away while the nurse removed the IV from her arm.

"You look much better and it looks like the baby has been quiet for hours." The nurse set the IV on the tray and then unfastened the strap around Penelope's stomach. "If they start up again don't hesitate to get back in here, okay?"

Penelope nodded and sat up with Vivian's help.

"I think you should go home with me tonight. I want to keep an eye on you," Vivian offered as Penelope adjusted her clothes and swung her legs over the edge of the bed. "The girls will be happy to have you there too."

"Are you sure?"

Amelia stood up. "You don't get a say. You're going."

Penelope nodded. "Where did Brock go? He never came back in."

Amelia and Vivian exchanged looks. "He has some things to take care of. You'll see him in a few days. Don't worry about him."

But she did worry. She didn't want him away from her, perhaps she should have made that more clear.

When she was released, Vivian drove her and Amelia to her townhouse where Sam had taken the girls. They were all sitting on the couch watching Frozen. The girls were singing and Sam looked completely out of his element.

The moment they walked through the door he stood and walked to them. His eyes scanned over Penelope. "Everything is okay now?"

She nodded. "False labor. I have to take it easy for the next few months."

"Why don't we just consider you on maternity leave then?"

Penelope shook her head. "I can't go without a job. The daycare isn't ready yet."

Sam smiled and rested his hands on her shoulders. "Listen, you have a whole family here who wants to see that baby. Taking care of you ensures that we're going to get to. I'm not firing you or kicking you out. But if you need the time…"

"But your mother isn't coming until December."

Sam looked at Amelia and then back at Penelope with a plan brewing behind his eyes. She'd seen that look exchanged between them before.

"I hired a new assistant. One that can stay on permanently. You girls can get the daycare up and running and when you're ready then, you'll already be in your element."

Penelope let her shoulders drop. She'd been replaced, but that had been the plan. Maybe he was worried she'd eat too many candies.

"I'd be happy to come in and train her."

Sam laughed. "You can come in if you want and make sure everything is done correctly, but in a couple of weeks. I want you to rest."

She nodded. That was a term she could accept.

Vivian stepped past them toward the kitchen. "I'm starving. I have some deli meat. Anyone up for a sandwich?"

They all followed and the girls raced by them. Penelope wasn't hungry, but she knew she was going to be fed. What she really wanted to know was where Brock had gone.

~*~

The home of Greg and Gwen Romero was buzzing when Brock pulled into the drive. The flatbed trailer his father used to move things was parked in the driveway. On it was, the couch Brock's parents had kept in the basement from as far back as he could remember. His bed had been disassembled and loaded onto the trailer along with his dresser and about ten boxes.

Family. He thought he'd be spending a lot more time with them, but things had changed.

Brock parked his truck in front of the house as his brother loaded another box onto the trailer.

"You're the only guy I know who calls and says, 'I'm moving, load me up', and the work is done," Mason scoffed.

"You driving back with me too then?"

"Hell no. I did most of this."

Brock walked up the driveway to where his brother stood. He rested a hand on his shoulder. "Thank you. I owe you."

"Oh, yes you do." Mason brushed Brock's hand away. "Mom's been crying all night."

Worry settled into Brock's chest. "Why?"

"She was used to you being deployed. Now you're making the choice to live somewhere else."

"I didn't mean to upset her."

Mason crossed his arms over his chest. "She's not upset. She's excited for you. You're growing up and that's hard to watch."

That made Brock chuckle and he slapped his brother on the back. "You're coming out, right?"

"We wouldn't miss it for the world."

~*~

Penelope woke early and wandered down to the kitchen for a glass of milk. She missed early morning coffee and assumed that that morning ritual wouldn't return until she was done nursing the baby.

That was something else she needed to learn about. How long was she supposed to nurse? How was she supposed to nurse? Was that really best?

Panic rushed through her. She was not prepared for this.

Closing her eyes, she took a few deep breaths to calm herself. It would all come to her and she had Vivian there to teach her everything she needed to know.

She looked around the small kitchen and noticed that on the kitchen table were the three boxes of letters they'd found in the attic. Everything inside of her itched to walk over and look at them, but she certainly wasn't going to. Vivian would never forgive her.

But she was curious as to why all of Adam's letters were stored away from Vivian. Why would someone keep them from her? And by someone, she was sure it was Adam's mother.

That panic rose in her again. Adam's mother would surely be making an appearance again, wouldn't she? After all, Penelope was carrying Adam's baby. She'd want to be a part of that.

The very thought must have made the baby a bit skittish too because Penelope received the biggest jab yet from inside. Though it hurt, it made her laugh too. If she could, she'd run and hide, she thought.

"You're up early," Vivian walked into the kitchen and straight to the coffee pot, which had already brewed a pot of coffee on a timer.

"I think I got enough rest yesterday."

"You're feeling okay?"

Penelope nodded. "Physically I'm fine. My head, on the other hand, is spinning with so many things."

"And the first thing on your mind is…"

"Brock."

Vivian nodded. "I knew that." She opened the cupboard, took down a mug, and filled it. "What are you thinking?"

Penelope shrugged. "Why did he just up and leave yesterday? I didn't want him to."

Vivian moved to the table and set her mug down before sitting in the chair across from Penelope. "He said he had things he needed to take care of. He'd be back in a few days."

"Okay, but why then?"

"I guess it had to be done then. He'll be back. He's a man of his word."

Penelope twisted a curl of her blonde hair around her finger. "He is. But what does that mean? He's only coming back because Adam asked him to?"

"I think you and I both know it's more than that now. Adam asked him to come. He asked him to give you his message and a few things. Of which I wish I'd known he had." Vivian gritted her teeth and Penelope thought of the watch Brock had delivered to her. "But I think he has some very deep feelings for you and that's why he's coming back."

"Is it too weird that maybe he has an interest in me?"

"Why?"

"Look at me," she said resting her hands on her stomach. "Who wants a pregnant widow?"

"You're not some reject."

"I suppose that would depend on who you asked. My mother didn't seem to want too much to do with me and you would have thought that being a single mother she would have embraced me and the baby, especially after Adam died."

"You haven't talked to her?"

"Not for months. She just doesn't have time for me."

"Maybe you have to make the first move."

Penelope looked down into her glass of milk. "Is it wrong to not want to?" She looked back up expecting to see judgment in Vivian's eyes.

"No. I can't say it is." Vivian sat back in her chair and sipped her coffee. "This weekend a friend of mine is having a barbecue. Why don't you go with us? I think it'll do you some good to relax around people."

"Oh, I don't know. I'm not feeling very social."

Vivian nodded. "Give it some thought." She looked at the clock on the wall. "I'd better get over to the old house. The phone line goes in today. We are about three days from taking applications."

A rush of anticipation overtook the panic that had sickened Penelope. "I can't believe we're almost there."

"Good thing too. I need a paycheck."

"What better way to earn one too? To be with our children all day—that's very special."

"You don't have to sell me. Those girls are my life. I'm ready to move on."

Penelope glanced at the boxes again. "What are you going to do with those?"

Vivian let out a breath, set her coffee cup on the table, and moved one of the boxes in front of her. "I don't know. I brought them home with the thought I'd dig right into them, but they scare me."

"Scare you? Why?"

Vivian ran her hand over the box that had once housed work boots and now held the unopened letters. "I hated him. By the time he died I actually hated him." She bit down on her lip and Penelope could see her cheeks grow pink. "What if these letters take that away and I begin to miss him? What if he hated me by the time he died too?"

That squeezed at Penelope's heart and she reached for Vivian. "I think he was confused. But I don't think he could hate."

Vivian patted Penelope's hand that rested on her arm. "Maybe I'm just afraid to stop hating. This is easier."

She supposed she understood that. After all, having been the last one that seemed to have still loved him wasn't helping in moving on either.

As Vivian stood and walked back upstairs, Penelope wondered where Brock had gone.

Chapter Sixteen

Penelope had opted to go to the old house with Vivian for the rest of the week. The girls opted to go to the rec center and play with their friends in daycare.

At the old house, which now looked much more like a daycare center than someone's rundown home, she spent some time decorating bulletin boards in the rooms of each age level. It had been decided, when they were at capacity, she would work the younger kids, the infants and young toddlers, and Vivian would work with the older kids. During the summer, they would have to think about even older kids. Maybe by then they'd be ready to hire someone, but as they hadn't signed up anyone yet, she wasn't sure how any of this was going to go. By law, they were limited to the number of kids they could have in each room. The house wasn't that big. But she redirected her thoughts. That wasn't the point. The point was to be with their children all day and make a living. That they could do.

As Vivian worked upstairs in the room they would make an office, Penelope continued to "cuteify" the room. When there was a knock at the door she peeked through the new front window and looked out to the front porch.

A man stood there with two little girls, one holding each hand. She set down her stapler and paper strips and walked to the door.

As she answered Vivian started down the steps. "Who is it?"

"I don't know yet. A man and two little girls." She pulled open the door and the man gave her a weak smile. "Can I help you?"

"Hi. I'm sorry. I didn't know if I should knock or not. I didn't hear any kids out back and I'm new in town. But I'm looking at facilities for my daughters for daycare."

Vivian moved closer to the door. "We aren't quite open yet. It won't be until next month."

The man's eyes widened. "Oh, I see." He looked down at his girls. "I'm a new teacher at the elementary school. Just got the job actually. I wasn't very prepared. Do you know of a center taking new enrollment? I'm kinda in a jam."

Vivian had passed right by Penelope now and stood in the open doorway. Her stance had softened and her hands slipped casually into her back pockets.

"I'll tell you what. Why don't you come in and look around? Let me tell you about what we will have here. My girls are currently at the rec center daycare, which will do for now. But then they will be here with me."

"You have daughters too? How old?" he asked and his tone was very genuine Penelope thought. Men didn't usually care, did they?

"I have a two-year-old and a four-year-old."

"Really? Charlotte here is three," he said looking at the little blonde girl with pigtails at his side. "And Stephanie is two."

Stephanie clung to her father and Penelope remembered being that girl. She'd never have wanted her mother to leave her side, but her mother would pull her from her and tell her to mind herself.

Vivian stepped through the door and the man followed with the girls still holding tight to his hands.

"I'm sorry. I didn't introduce myself. I'm Vivian Monroe and this is Penelope Monroe."

The man looked at them as if to compare them. "Sisters?"

Vivian let out an enormous laugh and tossed her hair back over her shoulder. Even Penelope had to stare. She'd never laughed like that before.

"Actually," Vivian looked at her. "You could say we were just very fortunate friends."

Penelope could feel the tears begin to sting her eyes. Vivian Monroe thought herself fortunate to be her friend.

"Excuse me. I'll let you show him around. I'll get back to what I was doing."

She moved back into the room, careful to wipe her eyes out of sight of Vivian's gaze.

She could hear Vivian's as she showed the man through the house. The girls had already found a few things that interested them and she could hear them playing.

But what stood out was the sound of Vivian's voice. It was light and airy. It was happy. It wasn't sharp.

When Penelope walked down the hallway to go up to her room, she saw them in the horrible little kitchen having some lemonade. Oh, there was something about this man that turned Vivian into a cream puff. It would be interesting to see if Charlotte and Stephanie were at the daycare on the first day or if the man would run from his job in Parsons Gulch.

It wasn't but ten minutes later that Vivian stood in Penelope's bedroom door. "Are you feeling okay?"

"Yes. I just thought I'd lay down for a bit. You know, doctor's orders."

She nodded. "Will you be okay alone for a little bit? I'm going to meet Clayton at the rec center and introduce the girls to my girls."

Penelope couldn't help but smile. "Clayton?"

Vivian's cheeks were blushed. "Yeah. He'll have to put the girls at the rec center for a few weeks, but he's decided that *Our Little Ones Daycare* is where he wants them to be while he's at work."

"Our first enrollment?"

"Looks that way. He just moved into town too. So I invited him to the barbecue this weekend too. It would be nice for him to meet some other people."

Penelope nodded. Someone had invaded Vivian's body, she was sure of it.

"I'll be fine here. You go," she laid back on her bed.

"Call me if you need anything."

"I'll be fine. Go." She laughed as she closed her eyes.

A moment later the house had grown quiet and Penelope drifted to sleep.

The bedroom had grown warm and that had awakened Penelope from her rest—and the sound of a saw and a hammer.

She sat up slowly and rubbed her eyes. She'd slept for quite a while. It was past two o'clock. She wondered if Vivian had come back. Until she'd heard the hammering outside she hadn't heard anything else.

The door to her room had been closed. Someone was there.

Penelope tied her hair back and freshened her face with a little water then headed downstairs.

No one was in the house, but when she looked outside she knew what all the noise was. Sam and Brock were both shirtless in the backyard assembling the play yard.

Penelope stood at the window and gazed upon the man she seriously thought she might not see again. His skin was tanned and that body—oh that body—was toned. She could see the flag tattoo on his side and the glistening of sweat on his skin.

She sat down in the chair beneath her in the kitchen and rubbed her stomach, lest she forget her situation and his reaction to it earlier in the week. He left, without a word to her—he left.

But it didn't stop the stirring his being there caused.

She looked out at him again and this time he was looking up at her. He smiled and even from in the house her body reacted to him. She could just ignore him and go back to hanging up bulletin board decorations. That's what she thought she should do, but her body couldn't be distracted.

Penelope walked to the back door and stepped outside.

It had been less than a week since Brock had seen her, but he was sure she'd become even more beautiful.

"Hey," he said as she stood on the back steps.

"Hello."

The welcome was anything but warm and he knew he deserved that. "What do you think?" He turned toward the foundation of the play yard.

"I think the kids are going to love it."

"I know they will. The coolest part is it'll be big enough for adults too. We could play on this," he said on a laugh, but she didn't smile.

"I don't see me playing on it." Her voice was cool as she rubbed her stomach.

Brock moved closer to the stairs where she'd perched herself over him. "How have you been feeling?"

Her brows narrowed and she glowered at him. "I was very much under the impression that you didn't care much. I mean you left me right in the hospital."

Okay, now he had to move to her. She couldn't think he'd just walk out on her.

"We weren't on the same page about things if I remember right. You seem to think that my saying I owe you meant I didn't choose to be here."

She pushed back her shoulders. "So you want to be here? I mean you want to give up your life to move to this little town to be here—with me?"

Brock began his climb up the few steps to stand level with her. "There's more to it than that."

She shifted from him slightly. "Really? Exactly how much more?"

There had been enough space between them he decided. He moved his hand to her hair and brushed it over through those blonde curls than hung from a tail behind her head. He'd missed the softness of them, those curls that usually framed that beautiful face.

"I have a place to live. I went back home and loaded up everything and brought it here with me. Even my parents' couch."

Her eyes widened and that was exactly the reaction he'd been looking for, so he continued.

"I secured a job and I'm even having a barbecue this weekend. I'd love for you to be there."

Now the crease formed between her brows. "I've been invited to one."

"Have you? By who?"

"Vivian."

He smiled and rested a hand on her hip. "Yep. That would be mine."

Penelope pushed her hands against his chest and took a step back. "She knew you were here and making some kind of residence?"

"Oh, they all knew. You just don't want to accept that I'd like to be here by you."

"Accept it? Look at me."

"I haven't been able to look away from you for months." He moved in again. "Be at the barbecue. Be my date."

"Date?"

"I'm not mixing words here. Penelope, I'm here to be with you."

"But I'm not alone," she said resting her hands on her stomach.

Brock moved in closer and rested his hands there too. "I wouldn't want it any other way."

There it was, the quiver in her lip. She was going to cry. And just as he'd planned he'd wrap her up in his arms and hold her until she stopped. So he did.

"Will you be there?"

Penelope nodded.

He pulled back and looked at her. "Okay then. I have to help him finish this. I hear you're already getting enrollments."

Penelope wiped her eyes. "Vivian said that. Some man brought in his daughters."

"She invited him to the barbecue."

"There's something about him. I've never seen her go so soft."

Brock laughed. He knew exactly what she was talking about. "I'd better get back. Will you have dinner with me?"

She looked away and then back at him. "I don't know if I can do this."

"Dinner?"

"No. Us."

"Let's start with dinner. It worked last week."

She actually sighed with a smile and he took it as a good sign.

"Okay. I'm going to go finish the bulletin boards," she said as she turned and walked back into the house.

Brock watched her. How was it possible he'd never wanted anything more than the woman who waddled away from him. Things wouldn't be normal for them—ever. They'd have quite a story to tell that baby. And he planned to be there for that.

Chapter Seventeen

Air-conditioning was Penelope's best friend, she had decided, as she brushed a curl from her eyes.

The little tables in the toddler room had all been set up and the tiny chairs pushed in. There was a rocking chair in the corner and a big round carpet with the ABC's where the kids could sit. They'd had to put plumbing into the room for a sink and a water fountain at the kids' level. And they all knew it was only a matter of time before they'd have to have more than a step up stool for the toilet. It would all come together.

They'd delivered the cribs for the nursery. They'd agreed on only a few infants, as there had to be a ratio between caretaker and baby that had to be met by law. Brock had promised he'd have the cribs assembled by Monday.

She rubbed her stomach as she looked at the little room that had once been a dining room and now would keep babies safe. Her baby would be there with her and he or she would be safe.

Before Brock even had made it through the back door, she knew his scent and his walk. She hadn't had to turn to see him coming toward her.

She closed her eyes as he stood next to her looking at the pile of boxes he'd set there.

"I can't believe this place is actually looking like a daycare center now. You girls did a good job."

Opening her eyes, she turned to look at him—gaze at him. His dark wavy hair was damp with sweat. His dark skin was pink from the sun and a bead of sweat still threatened to slide from his sideburn down his jaw.

Brock turned his head and looked at her. "Why are you grinning?"

"Am I?" So she was. In that moment of feeling safe, knowing she'd be surrounded by babies, friends, and cocooned in the house that was given to them she felt no reason to further be standoffish to him. "I was admiring the view."

That had his eyebrows rising. "But you're looking at me."

Things began to stir deep inside of her. She licked her lips and stepped toward him. "I happen to think you're a very nice looking man."

When he smiled that dimple came back. "I won't lie. I'm happy to hear you say that."

"I haven't been too nice lately."

He turned fully to her and ran his hands down her arms until he captured her hands in his. "You have a lot going on. I don't blame you."

"I just haven't been able to wrap my head around you wanting to be with," she looked down at herself, "this."

Brock unlocked his hands from hers and placed them on her belly. The baby wiggled inside of her as if he knew Brock was there.

"Whoa!" she sucked in a breath.

"She knows I'm here for her. Or he," he added. "Penelope, let me be here for both of you."

"I'm beginning to think I'd like that."

"I hope in time you'll more than like it."

She rested her hands atop his. "Don't you think it's too fast? I only met you."

"And how many actual days did you spend with your husband?"

That could have been an argument that had her spinning on her heels and running, but the truth had been spoken.

"You're right. I have actually spent more time with you."

"And I'm not going anywhere. Like I said, I have a house, a job, and a reason to stay."

"I'm your reason?"

"Both of you are."

That was all she needed. This man was of a special breed. She'd be an idiot to let him walk out of her life.

Penelope pressed against him and wrapped her arms around his neck. His hands came to her waist and she moved as close to him as she possibly could before she took his mouth with the purpose of letting him know exactly how happy she was.

It was crazy—just crazy. Her brief love and marriage to a man she didn't know had resulted in giving her a baby, two sisters of the heart, and a man—a man she knew she was falling in love with.

When the front door crashed open, they pulled apart. Vivian rushed in the door, the boxes of letters in her hands and the girls following quickly behind.

Tears streamed down her face as she hurried toward the back of the house. "Find something for them to do. Please, occupy them."

Vivian rushed by them and both Penelope and Brock looked down at the girls who were obviously shaken.

"I hung a tire swing out back today. You girls want to go swing?" Brock asked and two little heads nodded. "C'mon."

He gave Penelope's hand a squeeze as he and the girls passed. Yep, he was a keeper.

Amelia was walking up the front steps of the house and Penelope moved quickly to the door.

"Have you talked to Vivian?" she whispered.

"No," Amelia whispered back. "Why?"

"She's in the kitchen. She just ran in here with those boxes of letters and she's crying. The girls looked scared."

Amelia's eyes widened and she took Penelope's arm and headed to the kitchen. They both knew the letters had been opened. They were all in for a lesson it seemed.

Vivian was at the table and hunched over the boxes. Her shoulders heaved as she cried.

Amelia and Penelope walked cautiously into the room.

"You opened them?" Amelia spoke first.

Vivian popped her head up and her eyes fixed on Amelia. "Did you really think I could ignore them?"

"No." Amelia pulled out a chair for Penelope, motioned to her, and then took the chair closest to Vivian. "Did you read them all?"

"Yes," Vivian cried and rested her head against Amelia's shoulder.

Amelia patted her back and exchanged sad looks with Penelope. Vivian's hard exterior had been shattered. A broken woman now sat in front of them.

When she caught her breath, she sat up. Her eyes were swollen and red. Tears had stained her face and her hair showed signs of fingers having been raked through it.

"I sat down to just put them in order. I needed to see where they started." She pulled out the first letter from the first box. "This was the first letter he wrote to me after I returned home and went on without him."

Vivian handed the letter to Amelia, who read it and then passed it to Penelope.

It was awkward to look at Adam's handwriting and know that he had written the letter. She'd never seen his writing.

There was a stabbing pain in her chest when she realized that she'd never received a letter from him. She'd never seen his writing and never knew what was really in his heart.

As she read the first letter, she realized that back then love was in his heart. Pure love for this woman he'd grown up with and had fallen in love with.

The letter talked about how he missed her and wished she'd gone with him. He couldn't wait until he was home and in her arms again. It talked about having kids someday and even mentioned that he'd like to fix up the yard to the house they'd bought and take down that big tree.

The baby gave Penelope an enormous jab from inside and she sat back in the chair to give him some room.

As Penelope finished the letter she batted her eyes and handed it back to Vivian.

"All of the letters are like that one for the first six months or so. Then he starts to question me. He wants to know why I don't write to him. Why when he calls I'm so standoffish. By the second and third year the letters have no emotion to them. It's almost as if he's writing a journal entry."

"Why write them then?"

Vivian dropped her shoulders and pulled out an envelope from the second box and handed it to Amelia.

Amelia looked inside and pulled out the contents. "He was sending you checks?"

Vivian nodded. "He hadn't forgotten me. He wanted me to fix up the house. Once Emma was born he sent more." The tears were back and Vivian sobbed. "He was trying to take care of us and he thought I'd forgotten about him."

Amelia pulled her into her arms again and held her.

Penelope couldn't help but cry. It was comforting to find out that the man she'd married wasn't a complete bastard.

She rubbed her stomach and the baby moved against her touch.

Again, when Vivian could breathe and the tears had stilled, she pulled out more letters.

"Some of them apologize for the fights we had when he was home. In others, he asks me why his mother is the only one sending him pictures of his daughter."

"Why did she do this?" Amelia asked looking at the letters. "What could she have gained?"

Vivian looked through the boxes and pulled out another letter. "This one struck me as odd. After years of writing to me every day then every week, the letters came only once a month with a short note and a check. But this one came and it was much longer."

"He had something more to say?"

"He had a lot to say. It seemed as though he'd come into the knowledge that his father wasn't his father."

Penelope sat up straight. "Are you kidding?"

Vivian shook her head. "His mother had an affair and he was the product of that affair." She sat back. "I told you if Frank Monroe made a promise he kept it no matter what. He raised Adam as his own."

"That's horrible," Penelope's voice had grown higher. "Who the hell does that woman think she is? The rules to life apply to everyone else? She thinks she can just do what she wants and it's okay? Well, it's not! Adam's father should have kicked her ass to the curb. The nerve of her to cheat a man like that and to lie to her son. And then to do this to you. You were never a threat to her. Just to her ego."

She crossed her arms over her chest and leaned back in her chair again. She could feel the heat in her cheeks and her heart had kicked up its pace.

Both Vivian and Amelia stared at her and then both began to laugh.

"That's the grandmother of your baby you know," Vivian reminded her with humor still lit in her voice.

"Oh no, she's not. There is nothing that says I have to share my baby with that woman. And I won't. This is my baby. Mine! I'd bet Brock's mother wouldn't treat my baby like that and she'll be a good grandmother."

Both sets of eyes that stared at her grew wider and both women inched over the table at her.

"What did you say?" Amelia was smiling as she asked.

Penelope had to think about what she'd said. Then she realized she'd all but married Brock in one sentence.

"Oh," she sighed and rested her hands on her stomach. "I just meant…"

Vivian and Amelia exchanged glances.

Vivian looked out the window to where Brock played Ring Around the Rosie with the girls in the yard. "I don't think you could do better."

"I didn't mean what I said. I mean I like him. I really do. And he's nice. And he likes me. But I'm pregnant with another man's baby. My baby. My husband's baby."

Now her thoughts were coming as quickly as her heart was beating.

Amelia reached for her hand and covered it with hers.

"You were never married, remember?"

"So I just have some bastard baby?" The words came out inflicted with as much insult as she felt they'd been said with.

"No. That's not what I'm saying. I'm saying that your *husband* isn't coming back. There isn't any reason you can't move on."

"Out of respect," she snapped out.

Amelia smiled. "I've seen you two together and Vivian says she's seen you kiss him a few times."

"Sure but that doesn't make a life."

Again, Vivian and Amelia exchanged glances and smiled.

"You never know," Amelia said. "Maybe it will."

That didn't even make sense to her. Why did they even care? She would expect them to think she was some kind of hussy kissing a man while she was pregnant with another man's baby.

Vivian put the letters she'd taken out, back in the box. And just as quickly as she'd gone from crying to laughter she looked sad again as she looked up at Amelia.

"He'd asked me for a divorce before Ava was born," she confessed looking back down at the letters.

"He did?"

"He accused me of having an affair and he didn't think Ava was even his."

Penelope covered her mouth when a gasp escaped.

Vivian shrugged. "After finding out your own mother had an affair and a baby, wouldn't it cross your mind? And obviously he never got any of my letters and I never got any of his. It would look odd that your wife never communicated with you and then she was pregnant."

"Why didn't he get your letters though? And why didn't he say something? I mean obviously you two were together a few times. That doesn't make sense."

Vivian let out a long breath. "After he left his mother gave me his *new* address."

Amelia shook her head. "As in she gave you the wrong address."

Vivian nodded. "It doesn't match the return on these." She sighed as she rubbed the envelope between her fingers. "I guess my girls were meant to be in this world because he'd come home and we'd be in such a heat…" She trailed off and her cheeks grew pink. "A few days in, he'd want to know why the house was falling apart and what was he throwing his money away on. Of course that didn't make sense to me, so we'd fight."

Amelia leaned in toward her. "He never hurt you did he?"

Vivian's head popped up. "Of course not. Why would you say that?"

Amelia sat back. "Because I've seen it and that's why I trained those women. These men are sent away and moved around and you have to figure they don't know what's going on in their own lives. It builds up."

Penelope rubbed her stomach. "I guess his outlet was to move on," her voice dripped in sadness.

Vivian put the lid on the box. "It's over. There is nothing I can do. I can't even apologize or make things right. He's gone," her voice quivered. "He did tell me about you." She looked toward Amelia.

"Me?"

"After he asked for a divorce and I didn't obviously give him one, he said he'd met someone."

"And when I found out about you, I asked him for a divorce."

Penelope scooted to the edge of her chair. "So he really *wasn't* marrying more women?"

"He was. There were no divorce papers between any of us, and there was an enormous lack of marriage licenses too."

Amelia nodded as she thought about what was being said. "So it happened—exactly like you said it would. You opened the letters and now we don't hate him like we thought we would."

The three of them were quiet. Penelope wasn't sure she ever had hated him. But what she knew was she'd never even known him. The baby she carried was from a perfect stranger.

She looked out into the yard where Brock chased the girls around and they laughed. What harm would it be to give her baby another father then? Would Brock Romero want to take on something like that? Was he the right man?

It was true she knew him better than she'd known Adam.

Did he feel the same way about her as she did about him?

Maybe she would ask him what he thought about it. After all, they weren't starting out *normally* as it was. Maybe they could grow from a family into a couple. It was obvious to her that stranger things had happened to people she knew.

Chapter Eighteen

After Penelope, Amelia, and Vivian had gone through the letters it hadn't left much time for anything but a quick dinner since Penelope was obviously so tired and a little bit distraught.

"I should get you home," Brock remarked as Penelope yawned again.

"I'm sorry."

"I can't think of one reason you should be. You spend all day working on that house and you're growing a person. So you yawn during my dinner. Not something to be sorry about."

By the widening of her eyes, he realized he might have snapped that out a bit harder than he'd meant to. But he wasn't one to go for the overly apologetic woman. To her credit she'd been through a lot, but he wasn't going to have her be sorry for being pregnant and being tired.

Penelope fidgeted with her napkin. "I've been more tired lately."

"The baby is growing at nearly double the rate daily."

"Did your sister do this?"

Now he smiled. Who'd ever have thought he'd be the one dishing out pregnancy advice? "Yes. So imagine that she did this three times. I can't even imagine how she made it through the third time with two small kids running around."

"That makes me tired just thinking about it."

Brock reached his hand across the table and captured hers. "My mom was right there to help out. And of course she has a very attentive husband too. She made it because she had a support system."

He could see it in her eyes that she thought she didn't have that—an attentive mother and husband—and he wanted to make sure she understood that she did.

"You have Amelia and Vivian. And Sam," he added with a quick thought.

She raised her head and nodded. "I still can't believe I have them. They really should hate me and have turned me away."

Brock shook his head because he didn't believe that for one moment. "They are some classy ladies and one upstanding man." When she only nodded again, he let go of her hand and set his napkin on the table. He scooted out of the booth and walked to her side of the table to sit by her. He pushed the plates back and put an arm around her shoulders while taking her hand with his.

Her blonde curls hung to her shoulders and gave her a soft angelic look as she gazed at him with those blue eyes that haunted him in his sleep. "You also have me. Don't forget that."

She finally looked up at him and locked those blue eyes on his. "I've been thinking about that. Did you decide to stay here in Parson's Gulch because of me?"

She got it, he thought and he rested his forehead against hers. "Yes."

"Because you owe me?"

Brock closed his eyes and left his head pressed to hers. "No, because I began to fall in love with you."

Penelope pulled back and Brock raised his head to look at her. Shock would best describe the look on her face. Her eyes had opened wide and her lips had parted into an "Oh."

She processed it. "I guess that would be the best way to say it. It certainly gets your point across. You wouldn't have just made this decision if you felt obligated or…"

"Don't analyze it. And don't go shooting yourself down either. You're as worthy of being loved as Amelia is. And Sam loves her."

"She's not pregnant."

"And you are."

"That really shouldn't be a bonus point for a man."

"Maybe most men are stupid," he explained as he lifted his hand into her hair. "Give me a chance. Let me love you and the baby. I'm not going anywhere."

He could feel her begin to shake. How could she not have expected him to feel like this? He thought he'd been pretty obvious.

"What will your family say?"

"I guess we should find out."

"You can't just take home a girl who's carrying someone else's baby."

"Of course I can. And it's not like you're just some girl. And it's not just some man's baby. You're carrying your husband's baby—your husband who happened to save my damn life. Without him, I wouldn't be here and I'm very grateful that I'm here and I'm sitting here with you."

That seemed to stop the argument she wanted to have with him. Good. He didn't want to argue with her. Situations weren't always cookie cutter. It wasn't always meet, date, fall in love, marry and have kids. Sometimes things started for a couple in different ways.

"Would you like to meet my family?"

Her eyes were wide, but she nodded and that was a very good sign.

Brock moved in and pressed his lips to hers. "Good. They want to meet you too." He rested his forehead to hers again.

"Will you come home with me tonight? Stay with me," she offered softly.

Had he willed it so hard that she felt it burning inside of him, this need to hold her all night long?

"Are you sure?"

"Yes. I don't mean anything sexual by it, I…"

"I didn't assume you did." He pressed a kiss to her forehead and pulled back. "If I stay, can I hold you all night?"

Penelope went soft against him and rested her head on his shoulder. "That's exactly what I wanted."

The text message to Vivian telling her that Penelope had decided to stay in her own place tonight was responded with, *Be careful. Don't do anything you don't want to. Call me. I'm here if you need me.*

Penelope tucked her phone back into her purse as Brock pulled up in front of the house.

Illumination from the light on the front porch gave the house a welcoming glow. She was home, her home now. There was a warm joy that filled her when she considered that.

She liked thinking that she belonged somewhere and as she watched Brock turn off the car she realized it was nice to belong to people too.

It was a different feeling than when she "belonged" to her mother. Now she had people who cared for her, more than shelter and food. She had a family who wanted only the best for her—and her baby. And this man, this fall from the sky kind of blessing of a man, was falling in love with her and she'd certainly not given him any reason to. She'd reconsidered everything he mentioned to her. She contradicted all of his thoughts. But he was proof. There were decent men out there.

As he opened his door, she caught his arm. "Did you mean what you said back at the restaurant? You don't feel obligated to be here, but you're here because…" she trailed off.

"Because I was falling in love with you?"

Penelope nodded. At least he'd said it a few times.

Brock turned toward her, the glow of a streetlight filling the car with shadows and warmth.

"Yes. I mean that."

"Do you think when the baby gets here you'll feel the same way?"

He let out a breath and climbed out of Adam's Mustang.

Well, that wasn't what she thought would happen. She figured he'd put up an argument. They seemed to be good at that. She just wanted to know…

The door opened to her side and there he was turning her toward him. He took her hands and pulled her from the car, adjusting her slightly to press her back to the cold metal once her feet hit the ground.

His mouth came to hers in such a fevered rush that she reached for his shoulders just to hold herself up. Brock's tongue sought out hers in a fire, his fingers tangled in her hair, and his body pressed against hers—firmly but cautiously.

Penelope's fingers dug into the cloth of his shirt as he continued to kiss away any doubt that had built in her mind.

The doubt then turned into warm goo that must have oozed into her blood stream and coursed through her veins. And it carried with it the end of doubt. She had finally realized that she too had fallen in love with him and as the baby fluttered in her stomach, she was sure he too had fallen in love with Brock Romero.

As he pulled back, he kept his forehead pressed to hers. Both of them fought for breath that should have been offered by the cool night, but no, they still sucked in what they could because the passion between them made everything harder to control—even breathe.

"My mind isn't going to change. I love that baby as much as I love you," he said placing his hands on her stomach and the baby moved to meet him. "I think maybe she likes me too."

"I'm sure she loves you. Or he does. You're all he knows."

"Oh, I don't know about that, but I want to be who he comes to. I'm not afraid of it, Penelope—instant fatherhood. Or hell, just friendship. I just want to be here for both of you."

She wrapped her arms around his neck and kissed him hard. "I believe you. I think this is what you want."

"You're what I want. And I know that I don't owe you for saving my life too. For keeping me sane when I thought everything around me was ending." He pushed her hair back over her shoulder. "Adam gave you that baby. He spared me my life. He led me to you."

She'd been searching for answers from Brock from the moment she'd met him and she'd finally decided that she wanted him to be the man her baby knew—and she meant as a father.

He was the kind of man who would take care of and perhaps marry a woman having someone else's baby. He was the one.

Every emotion she could keep in check seemed to surface at that moment. Tears. Laughter. Happiness. But there was no sadness. Even knowing Adam had lied to her. Deceived them all and left her when she needed him the most—she wasn't sad. Because of him she was gazing into the deepest, darkest, sexiest set of brown eyes and she wanted him—Brock. She'd ask him to marry her after she met his family. She'd ask him to be husband to her and father to her child—their child. Adam gave him that power when he asked him to find her and he let go of his own life in Brock's arms.

And at that moment Penelope felt at peace with Adam.

Chapter Nineteen

She whistled when she was happy, Brock observed as Penelope moved around the kitchen preparing breakfast. Today must have been one of those days when she felt really good, he thought. That made him happy too. It was an important day and he didn't want her under the weather.

There were a million things to do before his barbecue that afternoon. He'd spent the past few nights in her bed in her arms and he should have been putting his house together. Instead, he'd helped Sam finish the play yard, assembled all the cribs for the baby room, and let Amelia kick his ass two more times. That woman was a huge force of power in a tiny little package.

On Monday, he'd start his new job and he hadn't discussed that with her either. He'd focus on that later. Right now he was going to watch her try to scramble eggs and make bacon. After that, he'd head toward home and set up his party. Vivian and Amelia had promised to keep her occupied and that was good. They too were setting her up for something special and she had no idea what the day would bring.

"I hope you like scrambled eggs," she said as she stirred them in the pan. "I'm no good at over easy eggs. I'm really not good at much more than this."

"You've heard me talk about my mother's cooking. I'm game for anything really."

She let out a hum. "I can't believe none of you have told her you don't like her cooking."

"Can't see a reason to break her heart. When you meet her, you'll understand. Taking care of people brings her joy."

Penelope's shoulders pushed back. "Is that where you get it? The wanting –to- take- care- of- people gene?"

Brock stood and moved to the cabinet where he knew he'd find plates. He took down two and set them on the counter. "Not a bad gene to have inherited. I'd say I got it from both my parents.

"I look forward to meeting them." Her voice was sincere as she scooped eggs onto the two plates he'd set down on the counter.

He was glad she was ready to meet them. Things between them were about to kick up a notch. He hoped she was ready for that.

Penelope sat on the back porch and watched Ava and Emma play on the new play set that Sam and Brock had built. Tomorrow the sandbox would be filled with new sand and as of Monday she'd be stationed at the daycare taking new applicants—and God, she hoped they had some.

Either way, Clayton had enrolled his girls and that was a start.

The baby squirmed and she rested her hands on her stomach. She'd swear she'd grown twice her size in the past two weeks, just as Brock said she would. But with Brock in her bed she'd slept better than she had in months.

When he'd drape his arm over her and rest his hand against her swollen belly, the baby would calm. She truly believed he'd love her and the baby.

Emma ran up the side of the play yard and quickly over to the slide. "Penelope! Watch me!" She called in her sweet little voice.

Penelope watched as she zoomed down the slide and landed with both feet planted firmly on the ground and her hands in the air as if she'd just finished an Olympic gymnast routine.

"That was great," she called out across the yard.

"Come slide with us."

That brought a laugh to the surface. "After the baby is born I will come and slide with you."

Emma fisted her hands on her hips and climbed up the two steps to the porch and to Penelope.

"When is that baby coming? She's been growing forever."

Didn't she know it? "Soon. Very soon. He or she will be here before Christmas."

Emma let her arms hang and Penelope thought she looked like a monkey with her lip out and her eyes wide. "That's—too—long."

"Not that long."

"I think it's a girl."

"Do you?"

Emma nodded. "I'll have two sisters."

"Maybe."

Emma walked next to Penelope and rested her hands on her stomach. "Is she moving?"

"She was."

"What's her name?" Emma asked as she repositioned her hands to try and feel the baby.

"I don't know yet. I like Gwendolyn. What do you think?"

Emma scrunched her face in thought. "How about Merida? Like *Brave*."

Oh, she should have known a Disney Princess name would sneak in there.

"What does your sister think?"

Emma motioned for Ava to join them. "What do you want the baby's name to be?"

Ava also crinkled up her face and gave some thought to it. "Dora."

"Dora?" Penelope thought that was old fashioned.

"Yep. Dora the Explorer."

"Oh," Penelope wrapped her arms around both girls and drew them in for a hug. "We will have to keep thinking on this."

Vivian cleared her throat from the back door. "What are you three doing?"

"Naming the baby," Penelope called back.

"I want Merida," Emma shouted.

"I want Dora," Ava copied her sister in responding.

Vivian shook her head. "What about Vivian? What's wrong with Vivian?" The girls laughed as they ran toward their mother. "C'mon. Time to leave for Brock's."

Penelope smiled as the giggling girls disappeared into the house and Vivian moved toward her.

"Need a hand up?"

"It wouldn't hurt," Penelope said reaching for Vivian's extended hand. She managed to her feet and then stood a moment to get her balance, her hands rested on her stomach.

"I carried Emma all in front. From the back, you couldn't tell I was expecting. With Ava, that was a different story. She liked to lie side to side, I guess. I was huge and gained forty pounds."

Penelope winced. "I'm at twenty-six pounds. I close my eyes on the scale, but I looked at the chart."

Vivian laughed. "You look healthy and with Brock around, you look happy."

"I do?"

Vivian nodded. "You do." She moved in closer. "He's treating you okay? I mean, I know he's sleeping here and…"

"That's all he's doing."

Vivian's brows rose in a look of surprise. "You're *sleeping* with him? As in not having sex but snoring in his ear sleeping?"

God she hoped she wasn't doing that. Was she?

"Yes, I guess. I'm not having sex with him. That would be awkward."

"Sex when pregnant is amazing," Vivian smiled. "Don't say you weren't warned."

"I'm a whale."

"I don't think he thinks so," she said as she turned and walked back to the house.

No, even though she said it Penelope didn't think he thought so either. But sex—that was something she'd have to give some thought too.

~*~

Balloons, cake, drinks, and food. Brock looked around the backyard of the little duplex that Sam had managed for him. What a deal. A place to live, a job, and a girl. And it all rounded out when he looked at the people in the yard laughing—family.

That family was only going to get bigger too. With no disrespect to Adam Monroe, Brock had decided he wanted that baby to carry his last name. Oh, he wouldn't hold it past Penelope to shoot him down. And who would blame her if she did. But he was going to bring it up, right there in front of his mother, father, sister, and brother.

"Brocky, this looks so nice," his mother's hand came to his cheek and she gave it a little pat.

"I want her to be surprised. I'd have brought her home to you but..."

"I know. After that false labor scare, I wouldn't want her far from home either. I'm just as happy to be here." She looked around. "Where is my potato salad? Your father must have left it in the refrigerator." She walked away to find her skillfully hidden dish in the refrigerator. Brock smiled. He was so happy they'd come.

Penelope's mother, however, hadn't responded to the invitation. That broke his heart. What mother just didn't care?

Penelope wouldn't be that mother. No matter her upbringing, she'd be fully attentive to her child. They both would be.

Amelia gave him a friendly nod as she and Sam talked to Clayton in the corner of the yard. He'd taken Vivian's invitation to the party, but when he'd shown up and realized a baby shower was attached, it took Sam's coolness to bring him down. It was informal, he'd told him, and that seemed to calm him.

Clayton's girls were already very involved with Brock's nieces and nephew in a rousing game of Ring around the Rosie.

Sadie found him near the punch bowl still taking in the group that was there. It was too small, he thought. There should be more people there for her.

"They just pulled up," she said to him.

He sucked in the air that had seemed to catch around him. "Okay. I'll go help them in."

He walked around the side of the duplex through the gate and toward the street. Vivian helped unbuckle the girls and they ran past him with a squeal. Vivian took a box out of her trunk and headed around back.

He moved toward Penelope, who had managed her feet to the ground, but looked deep in thought as to how to get the rest of her out of the car.

Brock reached out his hands. "Let me help you."

She took hold of his hands and he gave her a pull.

"I feel helpless," she actually whined.

"But you look amazing." He scanned a look over her admiring just how beautiful she did look. He rested his hand on her stomach. "How's our kick boxer doing?"

"He quit kicking once we got out of bed. Is this a sign? I'm going to be up all night long and have to work all day long?"

Brock smiled. "They seem to think so in the beginning."

Penelope rested her head on his shoulder. "Thank you for being there last night and trying to calm him down. When your hand is on me, he seems to know everything is okay."

Brock lifted her chin with his finger and looked down into those eyes he loved so much. "Everything is always going to be okay," he said brushing her lips with his. "C'mon, there is something I want to show you."

He interlocked their fingers together and walked her around to the back of the house.

Chapter Twenty

It hadn't skipped Penelope's attention that the street was full of cars and some of them had Missouri license plates. As they turned the corner, she quickly realized she had been set up because standing in the small back yard were at least twenty people, she only knew some of them from around town. There were balloons, food, and an enormous table of gifts.

Emma and Ava were running toward her with one of Clayton's girls, though she couldn't remember which one and another little girl.

"Pur-pize," Ava shouted and jumped up and down clapping her hands.

"Surprise?" She turned toward Brock who shrugged.

"Not just a barbecue, but a baby shower too?" His dimple deepened as his voice toyed with her.

"Really?"

He smiled sweetly. "Really. C'mon, there's someone I want you to meet."

Their fingers were still intertwined as he walked her toward a man and woman who were unmistakably his parents. There were parts of him that had distinctly come from each of these people and when they smiled at her, she knew he shared that quality with both of them.

"Penelope, this is Gregory and Gwendolyn Romero. My parents. Mom and Dad," he stopped on a breath. "This is, Penelope."

Emma patted Penelope's arm and diverted her attention. "Her name is the same one you picked for the baby," she said in a whisper, which everyone could hear.

Penelope gritted her teeth and smiled as she held out a hand to his parents, hoping they hadn't really heard

Emma's comment. His mother didn't even acknowledge the hand offered. Instead, she wrapped her arms around Penelope so tight that her grasp on Brock was severed.

She held Penelope at arms length. "Oh, look at you. You're beautiful," she said with tears straining her voice. "He said you were, but, oh, you're even more pretty than the picture."

She noticed Brock wince, but she ignored it.

"And look at this…" His mother placed her hands on Penelope's stomach and the baby all but leapt toward her. "Oh, he's a kicker."

"Yes. Especially during the night," Penelope added.

His mother moved in closer to her, as if to whisper in her ear. "We're very sorry about the baby's father. I'm very grateful that he saved my son, but I'm sorry he won't be here for his own."

Penelope's mouth opened. She didn't quite know what to say. They knew what had happened. Brock had told them what had happened and whose baby she was carrying and yet they opened their arms to her.

This was one of those moments when hormones and emotions collided and she'd break out into tears. She could feel them and yet she wished them away so they wouldn't see her as weak.

"I'm Brock's dad," the man next to her said and she turned to see an older version of the man to her side.

"It's nice to meet you. Both of you. Brock has told me a lot about you."

Gwendolyn smiled and tilted her head to the side as if she were admiring her. "He's told us a lot about you too." She touched Brock's cheek and patted it gently. "We're very excited for you and your baby. And we want you to know if you ever need anything—anything at all…"

Gregory placed his hands on his wife's shoulders. "I think we've overwhelmed her and she hasn't even met his brother or sister yet."

Penelope swallowed hard. She hadn't prepared for this at all.

Gwendolyn nodded and backed up so that the next woman coming toward them could say hello.

Penelope would have recognized her too. She was much shorter than Brock, a slender build with a little boy on her hip, but they had the same eyes.

"I'm Sadie," the woman said with moisture in her eyes. She flapped her hand in front of her eyes as if to fan away the tears.

She didn't even try to shake hands with Penelope, instead she pulled her in and embraced her, with the little boy, just as his mother had.

"I've heard so much about you. I'm so excited for you and my brother. Oh, and your baby. I'm…" The tears and excitement won out and she simply turned and walked away.

"C'mon. Why don't we go inside for a moment and get you a glass of water and let everyone settle in. I think Ava and Emma want to open presents."

Penelope looked toward the girls in their party dresses looking over all the big boxes on the table. She nodded her agreement to Brock, who led her through the back door.

When she was inside she let out a long breath. "I didn't expect this."

"You weren't supposed to," he said as he brushed her cheek with his palm and then slid his fingers into her hair. "Surprises only work when the person doesn't know about them."

She giggled at him. "You brought your family."

"I did. Mom didn't want you traveling after the false labor. And Sadie didn't want to miss the baby shower. Vivian and Amelia thought this would be a fun way to accomplish everything."

"They make everything better don't they?"

"They sure do try."

Penelope gripped Brock's hand, which was in her hair and moved it to her lips. "Your family seems to have the idea that we are together with this baby."

His eyes went dark and he lowered them. "I suppose that would be because that's how I've made it seem."

Brock lowered his hands and wrapped them around her waist.

"Penelope, straight out, I love you. I don't even want to pretend like it's something I'm just thinking I feel for a woman in a picture, or a woman I just met—it is what it is. And I know that I love you."

She batted her eyes against tears that stung.

Brock leaned in and brushed a kiss on her lips. "And, Penelope, I don't just love you. I love this baby. And I have from the first moment I saw his tiny body on that monitor."

"Brock, you shouldn't be saying all of this."

"But I'm going to, because I believe it and I think you do too."

She forced herself to look away from him. She had to gather her thoughts. When she turned back to him and his eyes were still gazing at her she knew what she wanted for sure.

"I had given some thought to this, and it sounds crazy, but I've known you longer than I knew my own husband. I've slept in your arms more nights and shared more moments with you than I ever did with him." She cupped his face in hers. "Brock, I don't want to be alone and I don't want to go through my life thinking that the only time I ever loved was fleeting and mistaken."

He lowered his head to hers. "Are you saying you love me?"

She closed her eyes. "Yes, I'm saying that and…"

"No, wait."

She opened her eyes and looked into his.

"Use the words," he urged. "I want to hear them."

She let out a sigh. "Brock, I love you."

His face lit up and his smile took over his mouth before he moved against hers. She'd never had anyone react to those words in such a way.

Heat swirled in her and everything buzzed in her head.

"I was hoping you'd get around to feeling that way," he said brushing another kiss on her lips.

"There's more."

Brock let out a breath. "More?"

She nodded and placed her hands on his chest. His heart beat under her fingertips.

"The baby knows you. I know that sounds silly but…"

"I think she does too."

Penelope smiled. "The thing is I want a family. I want to belong. With Vivian and Amelia I have that. But I want more. I want a man who loves us both."

"Penelope, you have that."

She nodded again. "I know. So what I'd been thinking about is this—would you consider staying forever? I mean, would you be a father to my baby?"

His eyes narrowed and he pushed back slightly. "That's what I want. I want to be her father, but I thought…"

"I'm not done."

"Oh," his dimple deepened. "Go on."

"I'm scared, Brock. I rushed into marriage and now here I am with a baby on the way. I don't want to make that mistake again."

"You won't."

All of this seemed too fast and yet not fast enough. Could she do this? Could she ask him to marry her? This was crazy. It was what she wanted, but did she want it for the right reasons?

"Brock!" A man's voice broke her concentration. "I'm ready to grill these dogs. I have a few kids out here eyeballing me."

Brock laughed. "I'll be right out," he shouted. "Mason, my brother. I didn't get that far yet to introduce you. C'mon. Let's stop hiding and enjoy our party."

He took her hand and began to lead her out of the house, but she wasn't done. She still had things to say. It had to be done. She couldn't have one more moment not knowing where the future lay with her and her baby. He wanted the baby. He loved her. This was right it had to be the right thing. Everything inside of her pulsed to tell him that.

"Brock, will you marry me?"

The words flew from her lips and he stopped walking and only then did she realize they'd stepped out onto the porch and everyone had heard her.

The air grew thick and her head began to spin.

Brock must have noticed because a moment later she was in a chair with him sitting right in front of her.

"You doing okay?" he asked handing her a glass of water that someone had handed him.

"Yes. I didn't realize… I mean I thought…"

"Don't you go taking back what you said."

"Right. What I said. I thought we were," she winced, "alone."

"You were focused, weren't you?" He chuckled and made her sip the water.

When she was done, she handed him the bottle of water and looked around. Every eye was on her. Heat crept down her neck and across her cheeks. His mother was crying and holding on to his sister who also was crying. Amelia's arm was wrapped around Sam and Vivian stood with her eyes open wide, next to four little girls and a stunned Clayton at the other side of the girls.

Penelope leaned in toward him and whispered, "Let's revisit this later."

"Hell no. I don't want to."

His words sliced through her. He didn't want to marry her. Not only that, hell no he didn't want to, that's what he'd said.

Oh, this certainly had been a mistake—a horrible, horrible mistake.

Brock stayed in front of her, kneeling on the ground. He turned toward his mother and motioned for her to come to him.

"Do you have that little gift I had for Penelope?" He asked with his brows raised.

Her eyes lit and she smiled wide. "In my purse. One moment."

He turned back toward Penelope and took her hands in his. "We can discuss this in just one moment." That flash of his smile twisted her inside and the baby rolled so that she could literally see him move.

She sat back in her seat and both she and Brock rested their hands on her stomach.

"Did you see that?" She shot out the question.

"I did!" His enthusiasm glowed on his cheeks and in his eyes.

"Brock, here." His mother handed him a small wrapped gift.

He took the gift and looked at it. "I wanted to give this to you when you opened all those presents. But you kinda need it now."

She sat up in her seat and took the box from him. Emma and Ava had inched up closer to watch.

Penelope tore open the paper and when it revealed a small felt box, her hands began to tremble.

"Go on. Open it," Brock urged.

Penelope opened the little box and when she saw the small ring inside she had to bite down on her lip.

Brock pulled it out of the box. "It's little, I know. But I wanted you to know how serious I was. When things workout, I'll get you a bigger one. I promise. I just…"

Penelope pushed a finger to his lips to stop him. "It's got to be the most beautiful thing I've ever seen. You were going to give that to me?"

"I was going to ask you and the baby to be mine. I didn't expect you to beat me to the punch."

"You want to marry me?"

"More than I've ever wanted anything."

"We're going to get married and have a baby? Together?"

Brock smiled wide. "There's no other way to have it. I love you."

She nodded. "I love you too."

He slipped the ring on her finger and stood, pulling her up into his arms.

With Brock's arms wrapped around her, she felt that pure love that she'd always wanted. They would be a family and she owed that to Adam, strangely enough. Maybe falling in love twice hadn't been so bad. With Adam, the quick fire of it had been lit, but with Brock it was a constant burn. But he wouldn't be there if it weren't for Adam. She'd have to make sure to thank Adam for that, in time.

Chapter Twenty-One

Once Penelope had stopped sobbing over the mixed proposal and the new ring on her finger, she finally met Brock's brother and sister-in-law.

They'd dined on burgers and hotdogs, and she graciously took a big bite of his mother's potato salad, keeping the delighted smile on her face as she forced herself to swallow it.

Emma and Ava played with Brock's nieces and nephew until his nephew fell asleep on Brock's shoulder. When it was time to finally open gifts, Clayton walked over to her.

"Thank you very much for having us today. I think it's time to get the girls home. They've been playing all day and we still have some settling in to do."

Brock shook his hand, but Penelope looked around to see where Vivian had ended up. She must have been inside because she didn't see her around at all. Wouldn't she want to say goodbye?

When she looked back at Clayton, his hand was extended and she shook it, only then noticing on his other hand he wore a wedding ring.

So, that would explain Vivian's distance from him all day. That was too bad, Penelope thought.

"I look forward to the girls coming to the daycare in a few weeks," she said.

"It's all they can talk about. That and Emma and Ava."

Penelope smiled. The daycare was going to be good for everyone, she thought.

As Penelope dove into her pile of gifts, Brock's mother had managed a seat right next to her where she could *oooh* and *awww* over every gift—most of which she had brought.

But the gift that had her heart nearly seizing to beat was that of a small outfit that had obviously been worn and was old.

She turned her head toward Gwendolyn, who was dabbing at her eyes with a tissue.

"It was the outfit Brocky came home in. I thought it would be nice for the baby to come home in it too."

There wasn't even time to react to the crying fit that took over from there. How precious a gift was that?

Penelope set the outfit on her lap and she and Gwendolyn were automatically in each other's arms. Her son had stepped in and stolen her heart and promised her a family and here his mother had completely cinched the deal.

Brock covered his mouth when he saw the reaction Penelope had to the outfit. Sam gave him an elbow to the side. "She's coming to Amelia's bridal shower, right? I mean we could use some great gifts too."

Brock laughed and so did Sam.

"I think they might be a little excited about this," he said watching his mother and sister continue to pile gifts at Penelope's feet.

"I've been watching them all day with their grandkids, Vivian's kids, and even Clayton's. Some people are just made of grandparent material."

And that was a true enough statement, Brock thought. His parents were made of that material.

A few hours later, Penelope's gifts were loaded into Vivian's car and Sam's truck. Brock had escorted Penelope to his truck to drive her home.

"I can ride with them. You don't have to drive me home," she offered.

"I'm going home with you." He opened the car door. "Currently, I have my parents, my sister and her family, and my brother and his wife sleeping at my house. I'd much rather be with you where it's quiet."

She laughed as she climbed into the truck and he shut the door.

As they drove toward home, Penelope reached for his hand and intertwined their fingers.

"I can't believe you'd planned to ask me to marry you."

Brock smiled. "I can't believe you didn't think I would."

"And all those gifts your mother brought for the baby. I don't know what to think."

"She's very excited for you. For us."

Penelope nodded. "Under the circumstances though, I don't know if I would have been so gracious."

"That's my family. That's how they think."

"I like how they think." She looked out the window. "I guess had I known about the party I could have invited my mother."

Brock squeezed her fingers. "We did. She didn't respond."

Penelope kept her gaze out the window. Of course, she hadn't responded. It didn't fit into her schedule. Penelope wanted to be mad. She wanted to call her up and let her know how disrespectful she thought it was to have just been ignored like that, but she found she really didn't care.

She had Amelia and Vivian—her sisters.

She had Brock—her husband-to-be.

She'd always have the baby—her baby.

And she had Brock's family. A loving mother *and* father who had already doted on her more than her mother ever had. She would gladly eat over-seasoned, hard potato salad for the rest of her life.

She turned to Brock. "How many babies do you want? You don't want to stop with this one do you?"

A smile instantly appeared on his lips as he glanced toward her then back to the road.

"I've always wanted seven kids."

"Seven?" Her voice rose with the absolute shock of his answer.

When he laughed, she settled into her seat. Then he gave her hand another squeeze. "If it happens, awesome, but I certainly don't want just this one baby."

"I want him to have your last name."

The smile on his lips was the unmistakable sign that she'd made him a very happy man.

"And what was that Emma said about the name you picked for a girl?"

She felt her cheeks heat. "She asked me what name I'd picked out and I told her I liked Gwendolyn."

"You have no idea what that means to me and you hadn't even met her yet."

"I fell in love with you. I was fairly sure I knew what kind of person she was."

They pulled up in front of the old house on Main and Pine before the others had arrived. Her heart was full of love for so many people. She'd never felt that before, but she knew it was something she could get used to.

She looked toward the house to get that warm feeling she'd get when they'd pull up in front an the porch light would illuminate the yard. And it looked as though Brock was doing the same.

"Did you leave the light on in the attic?" Brock wrenched his neck to look up at the window.

"I haven't been up there. It would have had to have been since we found the letters."

"Hmmm, guess we really wouldn't have noticed. C'mon, let's get the house open before they get home with all your loot."

Brock climbed from his car and walked around to help Penelope out just as Sam and Amelia drove up.

As soon as Sam stepped out of his truck he was looking up at the house. "Who left the attic light on?"

Brock looked back at the house. "We just noticed it. We figured we left it on when we were up there finding the mouse hole."

Sam shook his head. "I was up there yesterday boarding up a few more holes. I turned the light off. I remember because I fixed the light plate. A screw was missing."

They both looked up at the house and then quickly headed in together. Amelia stood next to Penelope.

"What's wrong?"

"They don't think we left the light on in the attic."

Amelia looked around. "You stay out here," she warned as she followed them into the house.

Penelope stood there unhappy having been left outside in the dark. When Vivian pulled up she too hurried out of the car.

"Where are they?" Her voice was quick and sharp.

"Inside. We left the light on."

"No, we didn't," she said, rushing past her.

The girls sat in the car in their seats and Penelope walked over and opened the door.

Emma was wiggling in her seat. "Where did Mommy go?"

"I don't know, honey. But I think she wanted us to stay out here."

Brock and Sam moved through the house quickly with Amelia right behind them.

Sam pulled his gun from the back band of his pants.

"You weren't kidding about the concealed weapon, huh?" Brock smirked.

"Not one bit."

Brock wasn't sure what Sam thought he was going to find, but he took a step behind him just in case. Amelia was quick on his heels and Vivian had run through the front door and up the steps.

She would have run right up to the attic if Sam hadn't held out an arm and stopped her.

"Go outside," he demanded.

"She's here. If not in this house, she's in this town."

Sam took a step back and moved in toward her. "What do you know?"

Vivian looked toward the illuminated attic. "She texted me. She said she was coming for us. She was tired of me keeping the girls from her. She was mad that she had been moved away from her home—her son. She blames me."

Sam nodded. "I don't want you to get hurt."

"Me? I'll kill her if…"

Sam held up his hand. "Don't say that." He looked toward Brock. "Let's go up."

Brock nodded. It had turned from a basic chore of checking out the house to an operation. Brock took a deep breath and closed his eyes. What a funny time to have a memory of gunfire exploding in his ears. The very thought of a sneak attack had his palms sweating and his heart rate kicking up. Suddenly the scar on his shoulder throbbed and burned. He opened his eyes and followed Sam.

Sam took the lead with his weapon drawn. Brock hadn't remembered the steps being pulled down when he'd left the house and that filled his stomach with that churning dread.

Sam ascended the stairs slowly. "Is there anyone up here?" He moved slowly and Brock held an arm behind him trying to keep Vivian from racing the stairs.

"Stella, come out! I know you're here!" She shouted from behind him.

Brock turned to give her a disapproving look. But there was a lot of anger inside of her. He couldn't blame her for being upset.

Sam cleared the top of the steps. "Someone's been here."

Brock stepped into the attic with Vivian all but pushing him out of the way. "She's looking for something. There is something else in this attic that we don't know about." She scanned the room. "But she's not here. Her perfume isn't fresh anymore."

If he didn't know better, he'd think there was a sparkle in her eyes when she'd said it.

Just then they heard the sound of a car horn outside. Those sparkling devious eyes of Vivian's turned into fearful black dots. "The girls. The girls!" she screamed as she shoved her way down the small steps of the attic and ran through the house.

Chapter Twenty-Two

Penelope watched all four of them run from the house and toward them.

Brock gave a solid yank on the car door before she realized she'd locked them.

She hit the unlock button and the doors flew open on all sides of the car.

"What happened? What's wrong?" Vivian was checking the girls.

"Someone ran from around the back of the house," she managed with a point of her finger.

Brock and Sam both took off in the direction in which Penelope indicated with Amelia right behind them.

"Did she see you?" Vivian checked over the girls and then turned toward Penelope. "Did she see you?" she asked again, her tone more panicked.

"No. I don't think so."

Vivian let out a long breath and dropped her head with a shake. "She's hurt us enough. Why is she doing this now?"

"From what you've told me I don't think she's right. I mean I think she has psychological problems."

Vivian's eyes went wider. "Ya think?" Her reply was sarcastic and Penelope frowned.

"Do you think she'll hurt us?"

"I think between Brock and Sam they'll make sure she doesn't."

"She couldn't have gotten away that fast from the house could she? I mean, she's old."

Vivian snorted a laugh. "Late fifties and a runner. I have no doubt that she could outrun Sam. Brock, on the other hand, I'm sure she'd never outrun him or Amelia."

Vivian looked around the car. "We should get all your gifts into the house and then you can come stay with us. I don't think she'd know where to find us. I never even told Frank where we were staying."

Penelope shook her head. "I have Brock. We'll be fine."

Vivian kept a narrow eye on her. "You don't mess around if she comes back."

"When they get back over here, we need to call the police."

Vivian nodded. "You're right." She looked at the girls who had, even through the excitement, fallen asleep. "I'm going to try and call a deputy I know. I want to keep this as quiet as possible. The last thing we need is people thinking that the new daycare center is going to have people breaking in."

Penelope dropped her shoulders. She hadn't really thought about that.

"Do you think we should not call them?"

Vivian shrugged. "Maybe we let Sam decide. But I want to know what she's looking for."

"Do you think it's that watch?"

"No. There has to be something else." Vivian looked up toward the house. "Something worth breaking and entering for."

Sam, Brock, and Amelia walked back toward the car.

"She outran you? Really?" Vivian scoffed at their efforts.

"I don't think it was a she," Brock said.

Penelope climbed out of the car. "Do you think this was some random person?"

"I don't suppose we'll know until we get upstairs and look around," Sam added.

"The girls can sleep in Penelope's room for a little bit. Let's go up there." Vivian bent back into the car and began unbuckling the girls from their car seats.

Sam carried Emma up to Penelope's room and Vivian followed with Ava.

When the girls were comfortable, they all moved toward the hallway.

"How will we know if they took anything?" Brock asked.

"We might not know what, but we can at least start to get a feel for it," Sam replied and then turned toward Vivian. "We need to call the police."

Her brows drew together leaving a deep crease in her forehead. "I will. I'm going to call Darby. Maybe he can keep this on the down low. I don't want it to affect the daycare."

Sam nodded. "I guess that's understandable." He looked up the steps. "Well, let's see what's up there."

Brock turned toward Penelope. "You stay here."

Penelope fisted her hands on her hips. "That's not fair."

He moved right to her, but the darkness of his eyes wasn't passionate or even kind. "You'll do what I say."

Penelope gave him a valiant shove with her hands. "You can't tell me what to do."

"Well, I am. And you're staying right here with the girls."

Penelope looked toward the room. She hated that she was the most likely choice to stay with the girls, but that didn't mean he had to treat her like that.

"Why don't you stay with the girls? I'll go see what happened up there."

He only raised his brows. "After your bout of false labor, you're lucky you're not at my place with my mother hovering over you. Now back down and stay here."

Penelope let out a grunt. "Fine."

"Fine."

"I'm not weak you know." She'd said the words but even she didn't believe them.

"I know. You're doing more than anyone right now just growing a healthy baby. So keep doing that," he pointed toward the bedroom, "in there."

Penelope let her shoulders drop and went back into her bedroom where Vivian's girls were sleeping.

Brock stood outside the door for a minute while everyone else went up into the attic. When he was sure she wasn't coming back out, he made his way up too.

Vivian was on the phone with Darby, who Brock assumed was a police officer and one she knew well enough to call on his cell phone.

"Okay, Darby is on his way," she said as Brock cleared the steps into the attic.

Amelia looked around the room then toward Vivian. "So who is Darby? And how come you know him so well?"

Vivian narrowed her stare on Amelia. "Adam and I grew up with him, if you must know."

"So he's a friend of Adam's?"

Vivian tucked her phone into her back pocket. "Was."

That seemed to humor Amelia and she crossed her arms, cocked her hip, and waited—as they all seemed to be—for the rest of that story.

Vivian finally dropped her shoulders and let out a ragged breath. "Fine. I was dating Darby when I met Adam. But that was forever ago and it really doesn't matter much."

"He still likes you," Amelia prodded.

"He's a nice guy."

"One you'd like to get cozy with now?"

Vivian launched toward Amelia when Sam stepped in. "You two need to stop that." He threw Amelia a look and then turned his attention back to Vivian. "He can help us?"

"Yeah. He's had a few run-ins with Stella too."

Brock hooked his thumbs into his front pockets. "What kind of run-ins?"

"She has a few DUI's under her belt. She doesn't know I know about them, but I do."

Amelia grinned. "What did his dad see in her?"

Vivian shrugged. "Now that I know about his paternity I don't know. What makes a man stay with a woman like that?"

When they heard a knock at the front door, Vivian walked back downstairs and the rest of them began to look around.

Amelia walked by the reading area near the window. "She tore all of these books off the shelves. She has no respect for anything."

"But the boxes in the corner are left alone," Sam noted. "That doesn't make sense."

Amelia looked closer at the books. "She not only tore the books down, she tore out pages. That's so wrong."

Vivian walked up the steps with a man well over six and a half feet tall. Even Brock had to crank his neck to look up at him.

He was extremely skinny with a pockmarked face and a toothpick clenched between widely gapped teeth.

Brock wasn't one to admire the look of a man, but even he could say Vivian had done better when she'd met Sergeant Monroe. Brock would admit, Adam Monroe was a nice looking man.

"This is Darby." She pointed a thumb toward the tall man. "This is Brock, Amelia, and you might have met Sam."

"Ya, I think we crossed paths a few times," he said slowly as the toothpick dangled from between his teeth.

"I think you're right," Sam added. "But the reason we called you was we had a break in. Someone was up here and they were looking for something specific."

"It don't look like much," Darby gave a slow nod as he looked around the room. "What'd they take?"

"As far as we can tell they only ripped through these old books."

Darby nodded again. In less than three steps he walked across the entire attic and was standing next to Amelia, who looked dwarfed by the man's height.

"Have ya touched the books?"

Amelia shook her head. "Not yet."

Darby pulled his cell phone from his pocket and began to take pictures. "So you think someone just busted up some books. Maybe the attic got rattled by that tornado a few weeks back."

Sam stepped forward toward Amelia. It was obvious she was about to go after the dimwitted police officer. Everyone had seen her fists ball up at her side.

"We've been up here since then. The house used to belong to Adam Monroe's grandmother. She had a reading area up here."

Darby looked around again. "Why?"

"Why does it matter to you?" Amelia burst. "What we need is some help finding the person who was in here. Penelope saw someone run out of the house."

Darby opened his mouth wide enough to turn the toothpick around in his mouth and stick it through a different gap in his teeth.

"Who's Penelope?"

Vivian and Amelia exchanged looks before Vivian moved toward Darby. "She's a dear friend and Brock's fiancée."

"Where is she? I'll need a statement."

"She's asleep," Brock said, his eyes firm on Darby. "She's seven months pregnant. We're trying to keep her calm."

"Fiancée, huh?" Darby shifted his weight to his other foot. "Jumped the gun a bit did ya? Knocked her up first?"

Now Brock's hands were fisted into balls at his side. Who was this guy? He was supposed to help them?

"Things are a bit different in the twenty-first century."

"Guess they are. At least Vivian had a solid marriage. Just like I do. Four kids."

How unlucky they were, Brock thought.

"Listen, I'm gonna need a statement from her. I'll come back by tomorrow."

That was much too soon for Brock. "I'll let her know."

"Darby, we want to keep this quiet. We're going to have kids in this house in a few weeks and I don't want to lose those who have already signed up."

"Heard about your business. Nice venture."

"Thank you."

Darby started for the stairs. "Who y'all think would do this?"

Vivian touched his arm. "I think it was Stella Monroe."

Darby thoughtfully took the toothpick out from between his teeth. "You're actually standing there telling me you think Stella Monroe did this?"

"Yes."

"You said that other girl saw someone run from the house."

"Yes. She saw them run down the street."

"Anyone go after her?"

Brock nodded. "The three of us did."

Darby ran a long tongue over that nasty set of teeth in his mouth. "The three of you ran after an almost sixty-year-old woman and lost her?"

When put like that they didn't look like the stellar athletes they were. Well—at least him and Amelia.

"She was far ahead of us before we knew she'd run," Amelia added.

"Right." Darby tucked his phone back into his shirt pocket. "Funny thing is, last I heard Stella Monroe was in rehab. But I suppose she could have gotten out. People don't like to be locked up for any reason." He gave them all a wave. "I'll stop back by tomorrow."

Chapter Twenty-Three

Sleep should have come easily to Brock. He'd hosted a huge barbecue for his family and friends. They'd surprised Penelope with a baby shower and they both had proposed to each other. But because some psycho had decided to break into the house—now his soldier senses were on alert and he didn't like that.

When gunfire was in the distance or there were bombs being set off, men didn't sleep well. When the scar where a bullet had lodged itself into your shoulder began to throb and burn, it tended to keep a man up pacing the floor. But when that man had the most beautiful woman next to him, snoring softly, growing the baby that Brock would father, he was so pissed that he couldn't sleep.

Part of him wanted to go upstairs and look around. Another part of him wanted to sit on the porch with a baseball bat and wait for someone to come around. And yet another part didn't want to leave Penelope's side. He couldn't deal with it if anything happened to her.

He'd wait out the hours until dawn. He'd keep touching her skin, holding her hand, caressing her cheek. The door was locked to the bedroom. The house was locked up tight. The tornado that had blown through a few weeks ago hadn't shaken the house. He wasn't going to let some deviant shake them.

Darby, no matter what an eyesore, would figure out who had been there. But it plagued him—Stella Monroe was in rehab?

As night finally closed in on him, Brock drifted away, but he drifted too far. Sergeant Monroe was gazing at pictures of his new wife with a smile.

"She's something else," he said with that easy way the man had. Brock had always thought if he had that easy way he'd have all the ladies. But he wasn't smooth like Sergeant Monroe.

"What's her name?" Brock asked as he polished his boot on his lap.

"Penelope. Isn't that pretty?"

Brock had thought so. But then they weren't in the tent anymore. They were covered in dust and the desert heat beat down on them and it alone threatened to kill them.

"On that ridge," Sergeant Monroe nodded. "Keep low and…"

The first shot rang out. Brock's head was clouded with the dust, the guns, the screams, and then the pain.

He was blinded by it all. His body thrashed against the ground. The pain was immense and it wouldn't stop.

"Hold still. Hold still!" Sergeant Monroe was there pressing something to his shoulder. There was blood. Lots of blood. Then it grew quiet.

When Brock's eyes opened Sergeant Monroe was still there. Brock's arm was bandaged, and Sergeant Monroe was in *his* arms—bleeding.

"Take care of her," he said as he coughed and blood trickled from his mouth. "Penelope. She's your responsibility. She's yours. They're yours to take care of."

The words grew faint until they were only an echo in the dark.

Brock sat up in the bed with a start. His eyes flew open and then winced against the sunlight in the room.

Sweat poured down his face. The pillow was wet. His hair was wet. His breath came in pants.

He was alone in the bed.

It took him a moment to remember where he was. That was until he saw Penelope sitting in the rocking chair clutching the bear the girls had made her.

Her eyes were wide as she watched him.

"Why are you looking at me like that?" he asked, not sure what had happened.

"You were talking to Adam. You were screaming for him."

"I was?"

She nodded. "You were screaming and thrashing around. I had to move. I thought you'd hit me."

He got to his knees and his legs tangled in the sheets. He pulled himself from the cotton prison and went to her.

She didn't let go of the bear and she didn't move toward him, so he approached her slowly.

"I wouldn't have hurt you."

Penelope nodded. "But I was scared."

Okay, he needed help. This wasn't the first dream. It obviously wasn't going to be the last.

"Don't ever be scared of me. But you did the right thing. You moved. That's okay to do."

She nodded again and then winced. "Those contractions are back too."

That was sobering enough to have him on his knees in front of her.

"How far?"

"I don't know. I was so scared that…"

He took her hands and kissed them. "Breathe. Do your breathing."

Penelope began to take her deep breaths and Brock moved only far enough from her to grab a shirt and put it on.

"Have you had another?"

She shook her head.

"Keep breathing." He moved to the bedside table where she had a bottle of water. "Here, drink a sip of this. Just a sip."

Penelope sipped slowly and then let out a breath. Her eyes closed and she kept breathing.

"I'm tired."

"Okay, let's get you on the bed and prop your feet up. Let's see what happens."

He helped her from the chair and to the bed where he lowered her down.

"I think I'm okay now," she said.

"You're exhausted and I think that's all my fault."

Penelope rubbed her hands over her stomach. "I think I was afraid someone would break in."

"Not going to happen," he assured her. "I'm going to get an alarm system and some new locks on the doors."

She smiled as her eyes drifted closed. "Don't go too far."

"I'm going to make some coffee."

"Okay. Come back up." Her words slurred as she fell asleep.

Brock wiped the sweat from his face. If they weren't careful around her she'd have that baby early—induced by stress and she'd had enough of that.

When Brock unlocked and opened the bedroom door, he could already smell coffee. He froze for a moment before his thoughts calmed. Whoever broke into the house wasn't going to make coffee.

Vivian sat at the small kitchen table with her hands wrapped around a coffee mug.

"Where are the girls?" Brock asked as he moved to the cupboard to pull down a mug for himself.

"They are on nap cots in the nursery room. I figured this was good practice for when we open and they'll have to start coming with me. I'll just throw them in the car and we'll head over here."

He nodded as he poured his coffee. That made sense. "Why don't you move in here? I can take Penelope and the baby with me to my place. I can drop the baby off on my way to work."

Vivian sipped from her mug and he could see that she was actually considering it.

"I guess that would make sense. You start working tomorrow?"

He grinned. "Yeah. Couldn't have told you that when I left that hell I was trapped in that I'd be settling in Oklahoma with a wife and a baby. Sam's a good man. I'm grateful for the job so I can provide for them. She deserves that."

"You're taking my job?" Penelope was in the doorway, her eyes wide and her hair still tousled from sleep.

"Haven't mentioned that yet, have I?" He chuckled.

"No."

"It was going to be a surprise and I was going to have you train me. But I think we've had enough surprises lately."

She agreed with a nod.

"Why are you up?"

She shuffled to the table and sat down. "Baby doesn't want me to sleep."

Brock set his mug on the counter and moved to her. "No more contractions?"

She leaned back in her seat and rested her hands on her stomach. "No. Just a restless baby."

That was okay. He didn't like all the contractions she was having. That worried him. He'd need to ask Sadie about that. He didn't remember her ever going through all of that with her pregnancies, but then again he wasn't around for all of them.

"I talked to Darby last night about midnight." Vivian sipped her coffee. "He said they had six calls of vandals around town last night. He figures we were just part of that."

"But they were in the house," Brock reminded her.

"I know. I want to go up there and sift through it," she added as she looked up at Penelope. "He wants to know what you saw too. Did you see a woman running? Because he says, Stella Monroe is in rehab."

Penelope's shoulders dropped. "I don't know what I saw. It was just a person and it scared me. I locked the doors and just began honking the horn. I couldn't tell you if it was her. But she texted you."

Vivian nodded. "Yes she did." She stood from the table and walked to the sink to rinse out her mug. "I'm going to look into this and find out where she really is. But now I'm going up to look in the attic."

Vivian started up the stairs toward the attic and Brock moved to Penelope, kneeling down in front of her. "I want you to go back up and rest. I'm worried about all of your contractions."

She nodded hesitantly and he helped her to her feet.

Once Penelope was tucked back into bed, he walked up the steps to the attic to see what Vivian might have found.

She sat among torn up, vintage books with a grin on her face. "Reading nook my ass." She held up an old copy of *Little Women*. The book had a huge hole inside of it. "I just found three hundred dollars in this book."

"She was hiding money?"

Vivian nodded. "Someone knew that too, because they were only targeting these books."

Brock looked around the house. "Do you think they got some of it?"

She nodded. "I think there was an old box under the books. It had a lock on it. It was wooden and carved."

"Yeah, I remember it vaguely. I didn't look at it really."

"They took it. I think they thought it was the prize and they happened to knock a few books over in the meantime and pages fell out."

"But that means it's someone who knew about the books."

She nodded again. "I'm going to call off Darby. He thinks there are just vandals. I think there is more to it."

"Stella?"

"Oh, yes. I'll find out if she's in rehab or not. I'll pay her a visit." She looked at the enormous bookshelves filled with books. "But for now I'm going to see what Frank really left us." Maybe I'll wait until closer to Christmas to pay her a visit. She always was sentimental around the holidays."

Brock decided he never wanted to be on the bad side of Vivian Monroe.

Brock went back down to Penelope's bedroom. She turned her head and looked at him. "Come sit."

"You're supposed to be sleeping."

"Resting," she reminded him.

He sat down on the edge of the bed and stroked her hair back. "Feeling better?"

"Yes. I just realized this baby will be here in seven weeks."

"Give or take. He seems to be fairly anxious to get here."

For a moment, she looked away. "I want Adam to be some part of this. I don't know how to do that."

Compassion. It ran through Penelope's veins and this was some of why he loved her. Hadn't she always been the one to step in between Vivian and Amelia? The girls loved her. His own family adored her.

"He is part of it. But he should never be forgotten. No matter what. Maybe you could use his name as a middle name."

Penelope gave him a thoughtful look. "I'm going to name her Gwendolyn if it's a girl. I really want to do that."

Brock smiled. "My mother would be honored."

"Maybe Gregory if it's a boy."

Now he laughed. "You won them over. You don't have to name your baby after them."

"Gregory Adam is a nice name."

It sure was. "Doesn't go too well with Gwendolyn though."

"Gwendolyn Monroe."

"That sounds like a movie star name right there."

Penelope rubbed her stomach. "You're going to work for Sam?"

"I am."

"He's a wonderful man. After Adam died and he called me and told me there was a situation, I never thought it would end well."

"Well, it has for you and Amelia." He nodded up to indicate the attic. "I think he left one of you still struggling to get a grip on everything.

"Is she okay?"

He laughed. "I think she's fine. She just found out all those books are hollowed out and filled with money."

Penelope sat up. "No."

"Yes."

"Do you think they'll come back for it?"

"She seems to think they came for what they wanted. There's some wooden carved box missing."

"The wooden jewelry box that was engraved with a heart and had some rhinestones on it?"

"You saw that?"

She nodded. "I wanted to touch it. It was so pretty."

"I hardly had noticed it."

Brock looped one of her blonde curls around his finger. "I'm going to head to my place in a bit and see my family off."

"I want to come too."

That made him very happy. "My dad has something for me."

"Oh," she sighed. "I can wait."

"It's okay. I'm sure it's my college fund. He used to joke that he saved all that money and then I went to play war."

She narrowed her brows. "There was no playing there."

"He knows that better than anyone. But he used to tease that he'd give it to me to buy a house if I ever met a worthy woman."

Now her eyes widened. "Oh."

"So I've been thinking. I told Vivian she and the girls should move in here. We could finish off the other bedroom on the floor and they'd have their own place. Then the girls wouldn't have to get up early to come here. And I could drop the baby off when you went to work."

She looked around the room they'd put together for her. "I'd miss this."

"But I think the girls would like it."

She smiled wide. "They would. We could make them bears too, just like they did for me."

He patted her hand. "We could do that."

She sat up tall again. "You'd buy a house for us?"

"Penelope, I'm never going anywhere. I think Adam knew that when he sent me."

She wrapped her arms around his neck and pulled him in close. "I'm glad he did."

Penelope sat on the back porch watching Emma and Ava play on the new play set with her fiancé. Inside of her grew a life that had bonded her to so many wonderful people. And in a few weeks that beautiful baby would be in her arms.

She had sisters, brothers, and a fiancé now. In one year, her entire life had changed and even with the bad had come good. Even in the dark, there had been light.

The baby kicked against her and she took a breath. They still had to deal with Adam's mother. But she shouldn't be a threat. If she, Amelia, and Vivian had learned to live together why couldn't Stella Monroe accept it? Perhaps that was too optimistic.

The breeze blew through the yard and she closed her eyes. She didn't want to think about Stella Monroe. She wanted to begin to make wedding plans and mentally browse all the baby gifts she'd received—they'd received.

She gathered the shawl around her as fall was becoming colder. When they told her Adam Monroe had died she never assumed she'd be happy again, but God she was happy.

We hope you enjoyed PENELOPE, book two in the Three Mrs. Monroes Trilogy.

Here is a preview of book three, VIVIAN.

Available October 2014

Chapter One

God she was miserable. Vivian Monroe sat in her car just on the outskirts of town. The late November wind was kicking up. It was cold and her damn car had stalled—just like everything had for her for years.

It had been less than six months ago that she found out her husband of ten years had married two other women before his death.

Never in a million years, though, did she think she'd make a new life with those other two Mrs. Monroes. Adam, her husband, had left her with nothing. His second wife, whom he'd left everything to, had stepped up to make sure that Vivian and her daughters were taken care of. She may never admit it aloud, but she'd learned a lot from Amelia.

It had been Amelia who had come up with the plan for Adam's widows to take what he'd left and start a business. It would help to take care of Adam's children and then no one walked away with everything. They were building a daycare center of all things. It would open next week if everything went according to plan.

Her mind shifted to Penelope, Adam's newest wife. Though Penelope was only ten years, or so, younger than her, she felt as if she were a mother to the girl. Penelope was eight months pregnant with Adam's baby. She needed compassion—especially from Vivian, who'd been through the process.

Vivian gritted her teeth and tried to start the engine again. Nothing.

She'd called for help, but it was going to be awhile. Sam, her late husband's lawyer and Amelia's new fiancé, was in court. Amelia had an inspector at the old house they were converting into the daycare center. And Penelope and

Brock, the man who had been by Adam's side when he died in combat and now was Penelope's fiancé, were in a doctor's appointment.

She was totally alone. Even her own girls were at the rec center daycare. That, she thought, was the only plus to the day.

The day trip to Oklahoma City to find out anything she could on Adam's mother hadn't turned up much. Stella Monroe, by all accounts, seemed to be missing.

Vivian hated that she thought it wasn't really a bad thing to have the woman MIA. But, it did mean they didn't know where she was and there was a great chance she'd be coming after her.

After Adam had died, her mother-in-law had, well, gone off the deep end. Her husband had even found it beneficial to move her to Florida and away from Parson's Gulch, Oklahoma where she'd made her home for most of her life.

Still, she'd texted Vivian weeks ago saying she was coming after her and then the house where they were building the daycare had been broken into. Things just weren't adding up.

Vivian smiled when she thought about the books that had been thrown around in the attic the night of the break in. They'd all been full of money. Six thousand dollars had been found in between the pages and in the cutouts of the vintage books. Adam's grandmother had stashed it all there. As far as she was concerned, when they were given the house and all of its contents that included the money too. Of course, now sitting in her broken down car meant it might have to be used for costly repairs.

Another car pulled up behind hers, but it wasn't one of the four people she'd called. She looked into the review mirror and saw Clayton North stepping out of his car.

Great. The one man who had turned her head in all these years had come to rescue her. He and that shiny gold band on his hand that she'd neglected to see the first day she'd met him.

Oh, she had to have looked stupid flirting with him like she was. What made her think he was available? And why did she care, except she'd gotten caught up in all this falling in love that had been going on. First Amelia and Sam and then Penelope and Brock. She was a woman after all. She could certainly blame it on hormones.

She let out a long breath and waited for him to come to her door. When he tapped on the window, she opened the door.

"It's so dead I can't roll down the window," she said, forcing a smile on her face.

"I brought cables. I'll give you a jump."

"Thanks." She popped the hood of her car and watched as Clayton walked back and climbed into his car. He drove it around the quiet road so that he was parked right next to her.

He popped the hood of his car as he climbed out. "It'll just take a moment."

He pulled the cables out of his car and walked around to the front of the cars.

Clayton chuckled to himself. "I always forget which way these go."

"Red ones are positive. Black are negative."

He nodded. "Right. You'd think that would be easy enough to remember."

Clayton went about connecting the cables and Vivian watched, then what he said hit her.

"You said you brought cables. You didn't just have them and saw me stranded?"

Clayton shook his head. "The gal at the front desk of the rec center lent them to me. I'd gone to get my girls and they said you'd called because you were going to be late. I told them I'd come get you."

Vivian nodded slowly, her stare fixed on this man she'd flirted with and even had invited to a private barbecue. She sickened herself. Though he did come without his wife. That didn't uphold his character very well, she decided.

"You drove all the way out here to get me?"

"Yes."

"Why?"

Clayton looked around and then back at her. "Because you're stranded."

She crossed her arms over her chest as much out of irritation as to shield her from the cold. "Just a nice guy routine?"

Clayton's sandy hair was blowing in the opposite direction in which he'd combed it, giving it a ledge. His brown eyes were narrowed on her as he held the last cord in his hand.

"No routine going on. I thought we were friends and you needed some help."

"Friends? I just met you a few weeks ago."

"Right." He winced. "You invited me to a party too. Friends do that. Even if they just met. Remember I'm new in town. I don't know too many people."

"Whatever. Thanks for coming out. Very strange, but thank you." She couldn't even stand the sound of her own voice as she talked to him. The first time they'd met she was giddy and gushy—not like her either. But now she was being crude and snide. More like her, she thought, but not nice.

He clamped the last cable to the side of the engine compartment. "Okay, go start your car."

Vivian walked back to her car and turned the key. The car sputtered and finally came to life. When she looked up Clayton stood there with an enormous grin looking down at two running engines.

That nerdy grin was making her insides gooey again, just as it had when he'd arrived at the old house looking for a daycare for his girls. Two of the cutest girls she'd ever seen.

It was stupid to be mad at herself just because an attractive, smart guy considered her a friend. And then there was the matter of fact that he was going to be paying some of her bills when his daughters attended their daycare.

She let her mouth slide into an easy smile as she climbed out of the car.

"I really appreciate you coming to help me out. That was above and beyond."

"I'd like to think that someone would help me someday too."

Cute and genuinely nice. His wife was a lucky lady—whoever she was.

Clayton took the cables off of the batteries and rolled them around his arm. Vivian slammed down her hood and he did the same.

"Amelia is with the inspector now getting everything signed off on the daycare. If everything goes well, we should be open next week."

His eyes grew wide. "Oh, that'll be great. My girls talk about your girls non-stop. They'll be glad to be around them all the time."

He was easy to look at and easy to talk to. She found herself wanting to do just that—stare and talk.

"How is school going?" she asked, remembering that he was a new schoolteacher in town.

"So far, not bad. I've been called Mr. South, Mr. West, Mr. East, and Mr. Northbound."

She chuckled and he eased his hip against his car, which only made him cuter.

"Third graders are funny like that."

"Sometimes sassier than high schoolers."

When he crossed his arms over his chest, she was reminded of that wedding ring on his finger. She didn't want to be that other woman to worry about.

Vivian pushed back her shoulders and held out her hand. "Thank you, Mr. Northwest, for helping me out today."

He grinned as he shook her hand. "My pleasure."

"I look forward to seeing the girls next week."

She turned back to her car and began to climb inside.

"Hey," he called. "I'm taking the fam out for pizza on Saturday night. That place on the edge of town with the video games."

She nodded. She knew the place too well. That was where she and Adam had spent many of their teenage lustful nights.

"Anyway," he continued. "Why don't you and the girls meet us there? We can have family pizza night for everyone."

Vivian swallowed hard. "They'd like that."

He gave her a wave as he climbed into his car and motioned for her to drive ahead of him.

She put the car in gear and started back down the road.

Looking back in her rearview mirror, she saw him on his cell phone. No doubt talking to his wife.

She was a big enough woman to be friends with him—and the wife. She'd been lied to and she didn't trust anyone, so this would be a good step for her. Trust a man she just met that makes her insides gooey—and spend time with his kids and wife.

Nothing seemed off about that at all, she tried to convince herself. He was just a good, decent man. He'd come to her rescue and his daughters would be in her care next week when her business opened.

But it didn't stop the fact that he was so handsome and she wished he was single.

5 Prince Publishing is proud to present *Rocky Road* by Susan Lohrer. Please enjoy this excerpt. You can find this book and many more on the 5 Prince Publishing site at www.5princebooks.com

Rocky Road
By
Susan Lohrer

ROCKY ROAD~Susan Lohrer

Wouldn't someone who really wanted to get married be a little more careful than this? Not that Ancy doubted Mark's intentions. He was The One. And she wouldn't nag him about it.

Honestly though, severing most of the nerves in his hand should've been enough for one week—but no! He had to go and whop himself on the head too. It wasn't like Mark to be this accident-prone, and he'd been getting worse over the last few months. Working too hard so he'd be a good provider, no doubt. That's just the kind of guy he was. She smiled, visualizing him in a black tux.

Focusing on her impending nuptials usually distracted her from thinking about whether she'd make department head. And lately, her impending groom had been more than enough distraction.

She checked the temperature of the paraffin tub. "This'll feel a little hot, but it'll help with flexibility." He grimaced as she dipped his right hand into the warm wax. Then he gave her bum a squeeze with the left one. "Quit it before someone sees us."

Since he wasn't dragging his feet—that much seemed obvious—why couldn't he stay in one piece long enough to put some professional distance between them?

"Mark, you've dropped a wall on your head, nailed your foot to the floor, and dislocated your shoulder. Are you *trying* to get out of our wedding?"

Whoops. She bit her lip and glanced over her shoulder. Outpatient Physical Therapy was crowded in the afternoon. The last thing she needed was for someone to overhear her in a lover's spat… with her patient. That would not only prevent her promotion to department head, it would end her career. Instantly. Working quickly, she covered the warm wax with a plastic bag, then slipped a padded mitten over the whole thing to lock in the heat.

If only there were a simple way to get around the patient-therapist dating taboo. But because her specialty was post-traumatic hand rehabilitation, she was the therapist most qualified to care for Mark's injuries—so she and Mark were forced into secrecy until he regained the use of his hand. "Well, couldn't you try to be just a little more careful?" She kept her voice to a low hiss. "At this rate, I'll be ninety by the time we even set the date."

"Aw Ancy, a few more weeks and this thing will be as good as new." He grinned and held up his thickly swaddled hand.

Yeah, right. She'd treated her share of injuries. This one was far from pretty, even though she hadn't seen it until after the surgery. His poor body. "Please just be more careful. I want to wear my ring on my finger, not on my necklace where no one can see it." She displayed her perfectly healthy left hand, its third finger perfectly naked. Did Mark have any idea how hard it was on her to keep this a secret? And not just from the department—from Jen, her best friend in the whole world.

Though she was the one best qualified to treat Mark, Jen—perky, sexy Jen—could have treated his injuries. But then Jen and Mark—not that she didn't trust him—but why create temptation by throwing her beefcake fiancé into the capable arms of her best friend? Besides, every difficult PT case brought her another step closer to becoming department head. She couldn't risk losing that kind of security, not when she almost had it in her grasp.

"Promise me you'll be careful."

"You worry too much." He looked so hot when he gave her that wink that said she could count on him no matter what.

"Mark, I'm serious." She added a stern, professional note to her voice as Doris Ridgewood, the department head—who was due for retirement any second—passed by. "You have to take some time off work to rest. If you don't, you'll never regain full use of your hand."

Doris nodded approvingly and continued on her way.

Mark leaned close. "It's kind of exciting, don't you think, Ance?"

"What is?" She checked her watch. Almost time to unwrap the hand and work on scar mobility.

"Knowing you'll be mine to have and to hold." He waggled his dark brows meaningfully. "This hand is going to make a full recovery, and you know what I'm gonna do with it."

She could feel the blood rushing from her extremities, and probably from a few vital organs, straight to her face.

Jen, between patients, was walking past. Had she overheard Mark's titanically not-suitable-for-work innuendo? She slowed. Cocked her head. Pivoted on her heels. Ancy's promotion slithered down to the pit of her belly as Jen marched up to her and pulled her aside, a thunderstorm brewing in her eyes. "Is this guy giving you a hard time?"

Fresh guilt welled up inside Ancy, and she was sure her cheeks were as red as if Jen had targeted her with a laser pointer. Jen didn't have a clue, and it made Ancy feel like a big, fat liar.

"I um, got something in my eye." Jen shot her a strange look. But it was the only thing Ancy could think of on such short notice. She turned away and pretended to wipe at her face. When she looked again, Jen was with another patient. Ancy had never kept a secret from her best friend before, and she was starting to hate the way it made her feel.

Maybe she should tell Jen and just get this whole thing off her shoulders. But then Jen would be obligated to tell Doris, and Ancy wouldn't blame her if she did. And she'd lose her job. Her watch's second hand swept up to the 12.

Back to Mark. The mitten, the bag, and the wax came off, and she began to manipulate his hand through range-of-motion exercises, bending and stretching all his fingers, careful not to apply too much pressure to the still-healing surgery scars. His hands were muscular. Strong hands, dependable hands. The hands of a man who would stand by her through whatever life threw at them. And he wouldn't leave her the way Steve had. The way her father had left her family.

"Nice technique, Ancy." Doris's voice behind her shoulder made her flinch. The woman didn't approach like a normal person, she *appeared*. Ancy had never once heard her coming. "Young man," Doris said, skimming over the floor and coming to stand beside Ancy, "our Miss Robertson is highly qualified in her specialty. She's one of the best."

Wow. It wasn't every day Doris handed out a compliment like that. Could it reflect an intention to recommend Ancy for the promotion?

"Of course, Fidelity General Hospital is soon to be blessed with a second, equally qualified therapist. He's one of our alumni. Your case might prove especially interesting to him." She glided away, and Ancy pictured Doris as a young, heavy-browed girl balancing a book on her head.

Her mind was racing. "Mark, do you realize what this means? It's the answer to our problems." Because an equally qualified therapist who didn't have her seniority could take over Mark's case without threatening her promotion. Then the bit about the alumnus sank in.

"Ouch, let go!" Mark's face contorted.

Ancy loosened her grip immediately and banished the unsettling thought from her mind. "I'm sorry." She returned to her work on his hand and whispered, "You can switch to the new therapist, and we can come out in the open."

She pulled the curtain halfway around the bench for a little more privacy before starting to work on Mark's other injuries. These weren't as serious as the one to his hand, and while she concentrated on deltoidius, trapezius, and rhomboideus major and minor, she couldn't help but notice Mark's build on a more superficial level, which was part of the reason she'd pulled the curtain. Half the staff would be drooling over him if they saw his bare chest.

As it was, all she could manage to say to him when she finished the examination was, "Looks good."

The curtain behind her swished open, and the scent of Obsession for Men filled her mind with images from the past.

Steven Stone. Steve and her, training together, working together. Steve, the only guy who'd ever made an effort to understand her autistic brother and had never made fun of him. Steve and her, in his fossil fuel–burning Mustang....

Steve... the second and last man who'd walked out of her life. A wall slammed down in her heart.

It couldn't be him. She made herself turn around. Her arm brushed the paraffin tub, and liquid wax sloshed over the sides. A distant splash marked its landing on the floor.

Her heart did that funny flipping thing that made her breath catch in her throat.

It was him.

#

Steve watched Ancy run away—from him?

He'd returned to Fidelity for one reason. For the job, he'd told his mother, and he meant to be department head no matter who he was up against. But though he was ready for a long-term career commitment, his real goal wasn't the job. He hadn't wanted to admit that, even to himself. Because it could be too late.

The patient, Mark Castellan according to the chart Ancy had left on the bed, stared after her too, an undisguised glint of awareness in his pretty-boy blue eyes.

Glancing at the chart, Steve noted Mark's impressive medical history. Either this guy was unbelievably clumsy or he had the hots for his therapist. Steve wouldn't put it past any red-blooded guy. But he knew Nancy Anne loved her work too much to risk her career for some muscle-bound Lothario. And he knew her work well enough to know she was good at what she did. Maybe better than Steve was. It wasn't just technical knowledge of physical therapy, Ancy gave part of herself to her patients, making them feel immediately at ease. Steve hadn't mastered that. It could just be a girl thing. Either way, he was confident they'd work well together.

Still, they'd looked awfully cozy before, behind the partially drawn curtain. Never mind, he knew her better than that. What had happened between them was surmountable. It had to be.

It all hung on his becoming head of this department, in this hospital, in this city. Where Ancy was. He was doing it for her.

"Hey," Mark said, his gaze turning away from Ancy when the washroom door swung shut behind her lithe form. One more second, and Steve would've been ready to push the guy's eyeballs back into their sockets. "Can you give me a hand with that shirt?" He held up his injured palm.

A grubby T-shirt lay on the bench. Steve picked it up and recognized the odors wafting from it. Sweat, mostly. A whiff of marijuana smoke. And Ancy's perfume.

He initialed the chart. "Not if you want to get back the use of that hand."

#

Maybe running off to hide in the staff washroom wasn't the bravest thing to do, but it was that or stay in Outpatients and introduce the man she loved to… the man she'd loved. Hardly a situation that would let her show her professional, capable side.

Not that she still had enough feelings about Steve to make her cause a scene, or give her cold feet. Since she was perched on the back of a toilet in a locked stall, and the chill of the tank cover was seeping into her gluteus maximi, it was really more of a cold bum situation.

Why was he back? He must have known how uncomfortable it would be for her to work with him. Especially now, when she had to be on her game like she never was before. Maybe that was it. Maybe he wanted to make her as miserable as she'd made him. Which she really did regret, but you couldn't undo the past. Especially not when you didn't even know what you'd done wrong!

"Ancy?" Jen's voice penetrated the metal partitions. Anyone else would have waited until after work to find out what was wrong, but not Jen. She had this bizarre radar that told her when Ancy needed her *right now*. Then again, maybe Ancy was just no good at hiding her feelings. "What's the matter, hon?" Jen swung the stall door open, pocketed the quarter she'd used to jimmy the lock, and folded Ancy into her arms.

What's the matter? What *wasn't* the matter?

"Jen, I don't know what to do," Ancy wailed, dampening her friend's shoulder, but Jen didn't seem to mind.

"Well, why don't you march right back out there and say hi to Steve?" Jen loosened her grip on Ancy and dabbed at her wet face with a square of stiff toilet paper. "You've moved on with your life, and I'm sure he has too. It's been a year, after all." She smiled, and the corners of her dark brown eyes crinkled.

Jen was right. Steve had surely met someone else by now too. Of course, it was probably only a rebound relationship, but still, it hadn't taken Ancy long at all to find Mr. Right.

Oh, it was torture. Jen was closer to her than anyone was. Not telling her best friend about her relationship with Mark was the hardest thing she'd ever done. Keeping it quiet at work didn't feel right, but if she didn't, she'd lose her job. She'd almost convinced herself it was just a matter of bad timing. Almost. But Jen and Ancy had told each other everything since they were three years old.

Everything.

"Jen, about Mark—"

"You never mind about Mark." Jen grinned. "You've been spending so much time worrying about him, you haven't been able to think about what's really important."

"Like?" Like telling her best friend the truth.

"Like a very nice man is standing out there wondering why you took off as soon as you laid eyes on him."

"I know, but I really need to tell you about Mark." This was it, nothing was going to stop her, and it didn't matter if she lost her job. A best friend came along just once in a lifetime.

"You've got to stop letting your work interfere with your *life*." Jen shook her head. "It would be different if you were dating him, but only a complete idiot would get involved with a patient. Especially here, under Doris's iron fist." She chuckled.

"Dating him." Ancy's voice was a faint echo of Jen's.

"I'm so glad you've got your head screwed on straight."

"Yeah." Suddenly, her decision to reveal her romance didn't look like such a great idea. "You'd report even your best friend for something like that, wouldn't you?" She wouldn't. Would she?

"You know what they say about honesty." That was Jen for you. But still, this *was* Jen, and together they'd figure out a way to deal with it. Ancy opened her mouth, and Jen immediately pressed her fingers over it. "You can't help every fool who crosses your path, Ancy. Now, get off your rear, go out there, and show Steve everything is okay between the two of you." She pivoted on her white sneaker heels, leaving Ancy with her thoughts.

She was twenty-six years old, hiding from her ex-boyfriend. In the bathroom.

Lovely.

And she was wallowing in said bathroom while the most perfect, most amazing guy, who declared his love for her on a daily basis was—

Steve! She'd left him out there with Mark—what if Jen was wrong about Steve, and he'd come back to pick up their relationship where they'd left off? What if Mark and Steve got into a fistfight over her and trashed Outpatients? It could happen. She slid off the toilet and skidded around the corner. She had one hand on the door handle when she noticed her reflection.

Okay, cold water on the eyes, wipe away the mascara streaks, and a quick run of her fingers through her hair. She'd moved up a notch, from disheveled to tousled. It would have to do.

She was an adult. She could handle this. All she had to do was smile and be professional, and everything would be fine. Besides, she was probably overreacting—a lot could happen in a year. And really, what were the chances that Steve and Mark would get into a fight over her?

Steve hadn't exactly looked complacent.

Fueled by a burst of adrenaline—but mainly guilt—she heaved the washroom door open.

Uh-oh. Mark and Steve seemed to be involved in some kind of macho glaring match. She had to separate them. Now. She pasted a brilliant smile on her face and increased her pace to a trot, like a blonde Baywatch beauty in rescue mode. All right, so she didn't have silicone implants that slapped her face when she ran, but she did have the hair.

Halfway to her goal, she veered to avoid trampling an old woman cruising past in a wheelchair. The woman huffed, but Ancy just flashed her teeth and swerved back on course.

"Miss Robertson!"

Ancy's shoes squealed on the floor. Doris was headed her way, black unibrow in full descent.

"What is the meaning of this?" She crossed her arms in front of her chest. Ancy had trouble not feeling threatened by the gesture, despite the fact that Doris's head only came up to Ancy's chin.

It was hard to ignore what Mark and Steve might be getting up to on the other side of the room, but she tried for a direct, serious gaze at Doris. "I was hurrying so I wouldn't throw off my schedule." Over Doris's head, Ancy saw Steve hold up Mark's shirt, then toss it down like a challenge.

Doris frowned. "I expect my staff to show more decorum than that."

"I won't let it happen again." Mark wouldn't tell Steve about them. Would he? Ancy's breathing was still fast, and her cheeks felt warm.

"Are you quite all right, Ancy? You don't look well." Of course she didn't look well. How could she look well when Steve was back, tearing her heart apart and flinging it all over Outpatients like confetti?

In a valiant struggle to suppress a nervous giggle, she came out the victor. Barely. "I'm sure I'll be fine as soon as I get back to work." A big grin. "Thanks for your concern though."

"Very well." Doris stepped aside, and Ancy continued at a slightly more sedate pace, conscious of Doris's gaze following her. Evaluating her. She gave her hips a little extra swing, hoping for a smooth gliding effect. Swish, left. Swish, right. Yeah, she was starting to feel like a department head already. Glancing over her shoulder, she saw Doris turn away.

Finally able to devote her undivided attention to Mark and Steve, Ancy hurried toward them. "How's it go—"

Her right foot implanted in something sticky, and the left one flew out from under her. The room performed a swift gyroscopic maneuver, and she was suddenly flat on her back, trying to figure out why her head didn't hurt. She looked around and deduced that Steve, in a lightning-fast reflex, had broken her fall.

Which would explain why she was nestled snugly against his rock-hard pecs. Her head swam with memories she'd thought were safely tucked away in a locked compartment marked Top Secret, Do Not Open. More than just her head was swimming.

Down, girl.

It would probably also explain the murderous expression on Mark's face.

"I am *so* sorry!" The heat in her face before was nothing compared to this. She'd be willing to bet even her hair had given up its natural blonde color and opted for a stunning shade of boiled lobster.

Spilled wax had spread into a giant puddle and was hardening on the floor around them.

"Don't mention it." Steve wasn't making any effort to let go of her. Pressed against his chest, she was surrounded by the heady scent of his cologne—mmm, they didn't call it Obsession for nothing—and the secure strength of his arms. Her mind was again flooded with awareness of muscle groups, and she couldn't help but compare Steve's whipcord physique with Mark's bulky muscularity. It was so wrong that being in Steve's arms again should feel so right. So why did it?

Finally her brain kicked in, and she gracefully returned to an upright position. Almost as graceful as Bambi learning to skate.

Doris glided past. "Your next patient is waiting, Ancy."

There was a gray-haired gentleman in the waiting area with his arm in a sling. "I'll be right with him."

Ancy looked at Mark. Professional. She had to be professional. "I'll see you again the day after tomorrow." She offered a platonic smile suitable for public viewing.

"Right." He coughed. "Our *appointment*." Was that a smirk?

"Good to meet you, Mark." Steve extended his right hand, and then offered the left one instead. "Whoops, I guess you won't be using that for a while, will you?"

Chest puffed out, Mark rounded the bench.

"Wait," Ancy said, "the—"

Mark went down just as fast as she had.

"Wax." Now it was Mark's turn to scramble out of Steve's embrace. His expression was less than pleased.

"Are you okay?" She rushed to inspect his hand, but Steve beat her to it.

"Why don't you go ahead with your next patient, Ancy?" He gestured toward the mess on the floor. "I'll make sure this gets cleaned up before someone gets hurt."

Without so much as a shoe-squeak or a swish of her skirt, Doris was back. "Is something wrong?"

Ancy glanced at her watch and saw she was running six minutes late. "Just a little spill. Steve's taking care of it." She turned to begin her next session.

"One moment, Ancy." Doris unfolded her arms. "I've rearranged a few schedules. Steve will be working with Mark from now on."

Had Ancy's face fallen off? Because if it were still attached, she'd be able to feel it, right? She bit her lip, which had gone numb. Or wasn't there. Who knew?

"All right." No! Not all right. It would've been so perfect—if it were anyone but Steve. She looked at Mark, who was standing again. "Well, I guess that's it, then. Take it easy with that hand."

"Yeah, I will." He slid his gaze sideways, and she couldn't read his emotions. "See you around."

One foot, then the other. Each step she took put space between Steve and her, but the distance had no effect on her out-of-control pulse. How could he have thought for even an instant that the two of them could work together? Even apart, they were like two sticks of dynamite with a single fuse.

His coming back had lit the fuse.

She wasn't sure she could make it through the rest of the afternoon without being a danger to the patients. Why had he come back?

She made her way across Outpatients and picked up the chart for her last patient of the day. "Mr...." First name,

Donald. Last name, Fu—there was no way she was calling him *that*!

The man turned his head, and a smile creased his face. "It's all right, you can just call me Donald."

She forced a weak smile. "Well, Donald, let me take a look at your elbow." She asked him all the regular questions, and ascertained that although he didn't play tennis, he'd given himself tennis elbow by overdoing it with a screwdriver. To remove any doubt, she pressed firmly on the joint line.

Don't think about Steve, just do your job.

"Yaaaaah!" Donald jerked his arm away.

"It's a little tender, isn't it?"

Donald's brows drew together. That was when she noticed the color of his eyes. The irises were ice blue, rimmed with indigo, and looking into them made her heart give a sudden lurch. She'd seen those eyes before, but only in pictures of her father—and in the mirror.

Get over it, sweetheart, you have to stop seeing your father in every blue-eyed, middle-aged man.

She laid a hot pack on Donald's elbow. Well, she got it on his elbow after dropping it on his foot, because her hands were functioning at around 30 percent. Not that they'd been injured, it was just that she was shaking and couldn't seem to hold on to anything. He should have just stayed away. She'd almost gotten her life back together, and it was falling apart all over again.

"Young lady, you look as though you could use a kind word." Donald's tone was gentle. And he had at least thirty or forty years on her—loads of life experience. Why not?

"Can I ask you for some advice?" She removed the heat from his elbow and gently rubbed her fingers across his damaged ligaments to align the scar tissue.

"What's on your mind?"

Steve. Steve was on her mind. And the way she'd broken it off with him, telling him she'd needed time to figure out how she felt. He was gone the next day. For the next few months, he called every day. Then their phone conversations grew further apart. After he stopped calling, she'd thought he wasn't going to come back. His number didn't work anymore. She'd thought she couldn't count on him.

But he did come back.

"Well, I made a promise to… a friend, and now I can't keep it."

"That puts you in a difficult spot, doesn't it?" At her direction, Donald flexed and then extended his arm. "Perhaps if you explain your dilemma to her, she'll understand."

She? Okay, she could work with that. "What if she doesn't?"

He leveled his gaze at her, the disconcerting blue of his eyes—there was no way her long-lost father would suddenly show up as a patient, was there?—intensifying his solemn expression. "A real friend will try to understand."

When she thought about it for a minute, she decided he could be right. Of all the things she'd shared with Steve, the fact that they'd been friends their whole lives, at least until the last six months, had to count for something.

"I'm glad we talked. I feel better." Ancy jotted down some instructions for Donald to follow for the next few weeks. "Now I know it's hard, but you have to rest that elbow. And don't be afraid to ask for help next time you want to build something—we all need a hand sometimes."

He thanked her, and she watched him walk away. It would've been nice having a father who loved her enough to stick around. Not having one really stunk. Turning away, she banished thoughts of her deadbeat dad. Life was what you make it, right? And Donald had given her some great advice.

Okay, all she had to do was explain to Steve that she wasn't going to get back together with him. Of *course* he'd understand. So she wasn't ready to get married last year—if he was as ready as he thought he was, he wouldn't have given up on her after just six months. What was she supposed to do? Any woman would've fallen for Mark and his gorgeous eyes and the way he gave to the community. Working with Habitat for Humanity said something about a man's character, right?

Once Mark's injuries healed, she could relax. Department head would be hers. And her dream, the one that had always seemed too far away to reach for—maybe it wasn't as impossible as she'd thought. Not for a department head. Things were looking up.

Ancy said good-bye to Jen and grabbed her purse from her locker. Then she saw the shopping bag hanging beside it. *The Ultimate Wedding Planner.* When she'd bought it on the way to work that morning, she'd thought it would banish all her wedding anxiety, streamline the planning process, and leave her free to concentrate on work. Hugging the book close to her chest, she leaned her head against the bank of lockers. The man she'd loved. The man she loved now.

She would not think of the way she used to feel about Steve.

She wouldn't.

Yeah. Not working.

Books from 5 Prince Publishing
www.5princebooks.com

Meet the Author

Damon Kappel ©2009

Bestselling Author Bernadette Marie is known for building families readers want to be part of. Her series *The Keller Family* has graced bestseller charts since its release in 2011, along with her other series and single title books. The married mother of five sons promises *Happily Ever After always*...and says she can write it, because she lives it.

When not writing, Bernadette Marie is shuffling her sons to their many events—mostly hockey—and enjoying the beautiful views of the Colorado Rocky Mountains from her front step. She is also an accomplished martial artist with a second degree black belt in Tang Soo Do.

A chronic entrepreneur, Bernadette Marie opened her own publishing house in 2011, *5 Prince Publishing*, so that she could publish the books she liked to write and help make the dreams of other aspiring authors come true too.